The Bordeaux Narrative

The Bordeaux Narrative

Harold Courlander

University of New Mexico Press
Albuquerque

Library of Congress Cataloging-in-Publication Data
Courlander, Harold, 1908–
    The Bordeaux narrative / Harold Courlander.—
1st ed.
        p. cm.
    ISBN 0–8263–0915–1
    1. Haiti—History—Fiction.   I. Title.
PS3505.0885B67   1990
813'.52—dc20   90–34181
                                                    CIP

First edition

Contents

Statement of
Maurice Morancy

I, Maurice Morancy, residing in the town of Gonaïves in the Republic of Haiti where I was born, testify as to the following facts. My primary occupation is that of planter and coffee merchant, and I am also a scribe of established reputation. Because of my schooling at the Lycée Pétion and my meticulous scribesmanship, people frequently ask me to draft commercial contracts and wills, prepare marriage documents, and write diverse letters for them. It is generally known that a volume of my poetry has been published in Paris, and a number of my essays on Haitian history have appeared in European periodicals.

Several years ago by chance I met a man of advanced years by the name of Dosu Bordeaux who had a peasant holding not greatly distant from Gonaïves. Some time after our original meeting, emboldened by long acquaintance, M. Bordeaux hesitatingly asked me if I would be willing to commit to paper some of his experiences that he believed might be of interest to others. I did not at that time believe his life could have varied greatly from the lives of other peasant farmers, known as habitants. Much preoccupied by my own activities and interests,

I did not give any serious thought to his suggestion. But our acquaintance continued, and little by little he casually revealed certain fragments of his story.

One night while lying in bed I suddenly realized that M. Bordeaux did indeed have something worth putting to paper, a narrative detailing how the habitants of the countryside must perpetually deal with the supernatural forces that continually impinge on them. Thereafter it was I who importuned M. Bordeaux to tell me his story in a chronological sequence so that I might preserve it in manuscript.

Whenever he could free himself from his work, he came to my house in Gonaïves and narrated his experiences as long as his time would allow. On occasion we worked into the night and it was necessary for him to sleep in my house. If too many days went by without my seeing him I became impatient, and sometimes I had my horse saddled and rode out to his small lime-plastered hut to transcribe more of his memoir. The more I heard the clearer it became to me that any tampering, restructuring, or literary embellishment could only succeed in distorting and detracting from the story. Therefore I have added nothing to the original, omitted little, and made minor changes only as required to bring M. Bordeaux's vernacular narration a little closer to written language.

Naturally I cannot swear to the exactitude of every event he described, only that he was always clear-minded, and that other back-country people have testified that events of this kind were commonly known to them. Furthermore, many of his encounters awakened my memory to things told by my own father and grandfather when I was a child.

I herewith certify that the chronicle that follows is the true substance of what M. Dosu Bordeaux told me in many meetings over a period of more than a year. The story is his. My contribution is basically the craft of writing which I acquired in my youthful years at the Lycée Pétion, and also my profound personal interest in the substance of M. Bordeaux's recollections.

Nevertheless, being a poet as well as a *commerciant*, I have been moved to add the following words as an addendum to the testimony I have given:

Though we cannot see it
Do not say it is not there.
Though we cannot hear it
Do not say it is not there.
Ancestors, where they are living, cannot be seen.
The vodouns who protect us cannot be seen.
Our progeny waiting to be born cannot be seen.
Spirits within rocks and rivers cannot be seen.
Yet do not say they are not there.
What we see of the universe is a small leaf
Floating in a pond whose edges are beyond our vision.

Maurice Morancy
Gonaïves, Haiti
14 September 1871

I

My grandfather on my father's side was a marron who escaped from the Bordeaux plantation near Léogane, and my grandparents on my mother's side were from a plantation near Thomazeau in the Cul-de-Sac Plain. I never knew my mother's people, but before my father's father died he told us many things about where he came from and what the misfortunes of his life were like. His real name was Djalan and he belonged to the Bambara nation. In his town of Jenneh, where he came from, he was a leatherworker. According to what he said, he was on a journey to a city called Ségu when he was captured by Fulbe warriors who took him north and sold him to Hausa people, and those people marched him to the sea and sold him to Malinke people, who sold him to the French. The French took him across the water and brought him to Cap Haïtien in Haiti, where he was bought by a plantation owner named Bordeaux who lived on Morne Rouge near Léogane. I remember all these things because my grandfather told us about them so many times.

All the slaves who came from Africa were called bossale, or wild, so my father's father was bossale. He was also a marron, because that was what they called slaves who escaped and hid away somewhere. Some of the marrons went to the cities, but they were much safer in the mountain country. According to what we were told, my grandfather first went toward Port-au-Prince, but as the city did not seem safe to him he went into the mountains and passed around that place and then descended into the Cul-de-Sac Plain, where he met other marrons and lived with them. They had a small settlement near one of the lakes where they fished. They could not have gardens because the French would be able to locate them more easily. They made small dugout canoes which they kept hidden in the tall reeds, and they went out to fish with nets whenever it seemed safe to do so. Sometimes they went at night to the plantations and stole supplies, but this was dangerous because it told the French that marrons were in the neighborhood. On one of these raids my grandfather found a girl named Familia who pleased him, and he brought her back with him.

The marrons did not find it secure in the Plain. When they heard that French soldiers were looking for them they abandoned their hiding place and went south into the mountains. It was not difficult to find safety in the mountains. There were many marrons there, but the French did not chase them because the terrain was too difficult. The marrons made gardens on the mountainsides, planting seeds they had stolen from the plantations. They built small houses and covered them with thatch and plastered the walls with mud or lime. From where they were living they could look down and see the city, if there were no mists, and also the Cul-de-Sac Plain which they had left behind. On a very clear day they might even see sailing ships in the bay.

My father was the firstborn child of Djalan and his wife, Familia. What I tell you now is mostly what he told me about himself. He was called Golo by my grandfather because it was a Bambara name. My grandfather named him after a great Bambara king. But my grandmother was not a bossale, since she was born in Haiti, and she called my father by a French name, Jérémie. My father grew up in the mountains, and he was a full-grown man before he ever went down to Port-au-Prince.

His first trip was difficult and dangerous, but it was not because of the French. It was because of the baka and other demons that haunted the trail. On his way down he passed near where Furcy is today. At that time there were only two or three small huts there. After he passed the huts he came to a place where two trails crossed. There was a big tree nearby, and he heard singing coming from that direction. He thought there were people under the tree, but when he went to see, there was no one. The singing was coming from inside the tree. He poked his walking stick into a small hole, and instantly a swarm of bakas came out.

How they emerged through the hole he couldn't say, because they were as large as human children but in quite different forms. One resembled a human being, but there was no flesh between his skin and his bones, and his eyes were like red fire. Another was in the shape of a grey boar with long tusks. Another was in the form of a cornstalk with hands and long fingernails. One was a snake with a head at both ends. Another, more human in appearance, had no arms, and his hands were joined directly to his shoulders. They were all jumping around my father, preparing to seize and eat him. Things did not look very hopeful, but just then an old man who was a master of magical practices came along. He carried a cocomacaque stick with him, and he rushed forward and struck at the bakas with it. They retreated in terror into the tree. The old man told my father, "You will have to carry a cocomacaque stick when you are alone on the road. It is the only thing there is that will keep you safe from bakas." My father said, "Thank you, papa. You have saved me." Later, after he returned home, my father acquired a cocomacaque stick, and he never went out on the road without it, especially on a long journey.

The trails were very lonely in those days, because there were not as many people then as now. After his first trip, my father never made a long journey alone, but only with a group. For the women the dangers were greater than for the men, for sometimes demons would seize them and rape them. If that happened, a woman would give birth to a demon-like baby, and she could never have a normal human baby without a special curing and purifying service, which was very costly. A family might have to pay two cows, or a cow and a bull, to the houngan or vodoun priest. Usually a bull would be sacrificed, or a bull and white chickens, along with cornmeal and rum and other things. Some women were never cured and just kept on having demon-babies. The demon-babies were never killed, because that would make the demon-fathers angry and they would send smallpox or some other bad sickness to the family. Instead, the demon-babies were taken to a certain wild place and left there. The mother would talk to the invisible demon-father, saying, "Here is your child. Take it. Have pity on our suffering and do not torture us any more."

When my father was only a very young man the War of Independence against the French occurred, and it went on for a number of years. But my father and grandfather lived so far away in the mountains they were not involved. One time a band of soldiers came along our trail collecting as many recruits as possible. They took some young men along with them. None of them had guns, only machetes. My father was away at the time and was not taken. My grandfather said, "Give me a musket and I will go with you." But they said, "Muskets? Where would we get muskets? Anyway, you are too old." My grandfather said, "Don't insult me. Machetes can't kill muskets. Bring me a musket and I will show you something. Tell General Dessalines what I told you." They said, "Yes, Papa, we'll tell him" He said, "If you are afraid to tell him, take me to his house and I'll tell him myself." They said, "Yes, Papa," and went away.

There were some gardens on the other side of our mountain, and women and girls were taking care of them. The way it was done, the men hoed and cleared the ground and then the women and girls planted and tended the gardens. My father visited those people sometimes, and he was attracted very much to a girl named Ti Lena. Finally he brought her home and married her, and she became my mother. When I was born, in the time of Henry Christophe and Alexander Pétion, the war against the French was finished. I was the third child, the first two being girl twins. That made me a dosu, which is what the first child after twins is called if he is a boy. There were three more children after me, but two of them died while they were still infants.

What I am going to tell you is what I myself experienced and observed. It is my own story, not my father telling it or my grandfather telling it, but myself, Dosu Bordeaux, Bordeaux being the name of the plantation from which my grandfather escaped.

One reason my grandfather Djalan made his house and garden where he did was that there was a good spring close by. The water came out of the rocks and flowed downhill, finally dripping over a cliff. There were other springs also on the mountain, but my grandfather's was the best. Not only did water come from the spring, but sometimes the voices of spirit beings and our ancestors as well. The reason for that was that all our spirit beings, whom we called vodouns or loa, lived under the water somewhere, not just particular pieces of water like springs and lakes and the sea, but all water. When ordinary human beings died, if the proper rituals were conducted for them they also went to live below the water. If we wanted to entice vodouns or our ancestral spirits to visit us on certain occasions we would pour a narrow trail of water from the spring right up to the place we wanted them to visit. We called that trail the water road. We would have a dance and sing special songs, calling for certain vodouns or ancestors to come. If the spirit beings accepted, they would emerge from the spring and come along the water road, and when they arrived at the end they would leap into the heads of certain men and women and take control of them.

One time I was sitting by our spring and I heard voices coming from it. At first I wanted to run away, but then I decided to stay and listen. It was hard to tell what the voices were saying, because it sounded as if many people were talking at the same time. But it seemed to me that I heard one voice saying, "Dosu, Dosu." Because that was my name it frightened me, and I ran to tell my father. He was not home, but my mother was working in the garden and so I went to her and told what had happened. She said, "Do not be afraid. It is one of the old people greeting you." Later my father went to the spring, and when he came back a long while later he said, "Yes, they are greeting everyone, but particularly Dosu. He will have a fortunate life if he remembers to serve the ancestors and vodouns every year." I was too young to understand how to serve them, but I learned as I grew older.

One year the water stopped flowing from the spring. This was very bad, not only because we needed water but because it meant, according to my mother, that the spirit beings had turned away from us. My father and grandfather agreed. Because it was my grandfather who had found the spring in the beginning, he was the one who had to go to talk to the divining man, a houngan who lived some distance down the mountainside. He took a white chicken, bound its legs, and gave it to me to carry. Then the two of us descended until we came to the diviner's house.

This man's name was Kuku Cabrit, and it was said his father belonged to the Nago nation. He had a garden near his house, and it was generally tended by his wife and daughter. Kuku Cabrit also had another garden some distance away. He had a second wife who lived there and took care of things for him. He divided his time between his wives, but at the house of his first wife he had a special room where he divined and performed mystical services for people. My grandfather greeted him, saying, "Good morning, filelikela." Kuku Cabrit said, "Good morning, younger brother," which seemed strange to me because my grandfather was really very much older, but he did not take any offense. Kuku Cabrit said, "Why do you call me filelikela? I am a houngan." My grandfather answered, "Why, it is all the same. In my nation we use the term filelikela. If you divine and perform mystical services you are a filelikela." Kuku Cabrit said, "I divine. What do you want?" My grandfather gave him the chicken and told him about the drying up of the spring.

They sat on a grass mat on the floor facing each other, and Kuku Cabrit put his divining objects in front of him. First he picked up his gembo, which was a sea shell that slid on a cord. He fastened one end of the cord to his big toe and held the other end tightly in his hand. He slid the shell to the center of the cord and talked to it in a language I did not understand. He seemed to be asking questions, and in response the shell began sliding up and down on the cord. After a while he put the gembo down, saying, "We must go to the Ifa tray for more answers." He placed a wooden tray in front of him and threw small nuts on it over and over again. Finally he said, "Yes, now it is clear."

My grandfather waited for more, but Kuku Cabrit appeared to be thinking deeply. At last Kuku Cabrit spoke. He said, "You have an enemy." My grandfather said, "I did not know it." Kuku Cabrit said, "He is the grandson of the man from whose plantation you once escaped." My grandfather was surprised and said, "What does he want with me? I never knew him." Kuku Cabrit answered, "I cannot tell you that." My grandfather said, "Why, how is it possible? Since the revolution, all the French are gone." Kuku Cabrit said, "Yes, but in France the grandson lives, and he has launched evil medicine against you." My grandfather was still surprised and he asked, "Across the sea?" Kuku Cabrit said, "Yes, it is very powerful medicine."

After a while my grandfather said, "What can be done to get my water back?" Kuku Cabrit replied, "We will send an expedition against him. Come back in four days. I will prepare everything." We left Kuku Cabrit and on the way home I asked my grandfather, "How will we send an expedition? Do we have soldiers, or a ship?" My grandfather said, "What he spoke about has deep meanings. We will know in four days."

On the fourth day my grandfather selected another chicken and gave it to me to carry. We returned to the house of Kuku Cabrit. My grandfather gave him the chicken. Kuku Cabrit said, "Let us go where the big rock is standing." We went there and saw that the houngan had dug a hole as deep as the length of his arm. He attached a cord to a tree branch overhead. Then he tied the other end to a medicine packet, which he let dangle in the hole. The packet was wrapped in red cloth and was decorated with white chicken feathers and several copper coins. Kuku Cabrit sat next to the hole and shook a small gourd rattle. He sang, but I could not understand most of the words.

Several times I recognized my grandfather's name, Djalan, but nothing else. Several times Kuku Cabrit poured a little water into the hole, calling out, "Ogoun, Ogoun, Ogoun." He sprinkled some cornmeal in the hole and poured in some rum. After that he said, "It is finished. I have sent the expedition to France. My house spirit, Ogoun, has agreed to go. But France is a long way and it will take time. We will have to wait."

My grandfather asked, "What will Ogoun do?" Kuku Cabrit said, "When he arrives there he will enter the head of your enemy. He will torment him until he agrees to undo the evil force working for him. If your enemy sent a baka from France, he will have to call him home. If he used a medicine packet, he will destroy it. That is all. Now we are finished." Kuku Cabrit gave my grandfather some powder wrapped in a leaf and told him to sprinkle some of this powder in the spring.

On our way home I asked my grandfather if the water would ever come back. He said, "I cannot tell. If Kuku Cabrit is a good filelikela our spring will flow again. When the time comes, we will know." After that, whenever I could I went to the spring to see if the water was flowing, but after a while I tired of it and did not go any more. We dug holes in the ground and collected rainwater to drink. One morning my father came running to the house, calling out, "Water is dripping over the cliff." We hurried to the spring and found it flowing. My grandfather said, "It is clear that Kuku Cabrit is a good filelikela." He sent me down the mountain to tell Kuku Cabrit, who said, "Yes, that is good. Tell them to come sixteen days from now, and to bring three chickens."

We went to the service on the sixteenth day. There were drummers and many singers and dancers in the courtyard. The drums were decorated with pieces of red cloth and Kuku Cabrit wore a red shirt. Late in the evening the Ogoun spirit entered the heads of a number of dancers. It came into my mother's head also. She lurched and staggered and jumped into a fire near the court, treading the coals with her bare feet. Some of the people took her into the house. When she came out she was wearing a red shirt like Kuku Cabrit's, and held a very long machete in her hand and waved it like a sword. She was speaking a strange language. She seized one of the chickens we had brought and cut its throat, dripping the blood in the center of the courtyard. People sang and clapped their hands. Then she became limp and fell on the ground, lying as if she were sleeping. People took her back into the house, and Kuku Cabrit announced that Ogoun was very pleased with the service. When we went home the sun was just rising.

Another time this houngan, whom my grandfather always called a filelikela, worked for us was after a big storm came to the mountains and lightning struck a tall tree near our house. When the storm was over, my father went out and saw that the tree was split all the way down one side, and he began looking on the ground for the thunder stone that had caused the damage. I helped him look for the stone, but we didn't find anything. Thunder stones were smooth and black, with a point at one end and a polished cutting edge at the other. According to what I heard from my father and mother, the vodoun spirit named Hevioso hurled these stones to punish or warn people if he was displeased about anything. Some people called him Shango and referred to the stones as Shango stones. Since the stone had hit the tree and not our house, it seemed to be a warning rather than a punishment. But my father didn't know what the warning was about, and he was supposed to take the stone to a houngan to find out what it meant.

So we kept looking. Some days later my father found it in the earth while he was hoeing his garden. He left at once and went down to see Kuku Cabrit, taking a chicken with him to pay for the divining work. When he returned, he told us that Kuku Cabrit had consulted his divining nuts and found out that Hevioso was angry with us because we had not held a service for him in our house, which we were supposed to do. My father arranged for the service, but it was difficult because we had to sacrifice a bull, which we did not own. We did not have enough chickens to buy a bull, so my father began to go from one habitation to another for help. He would go to a certain habitant and persuade him to negotiate a par-preté, a share loan. The man would give him two or three chickens on the condition that my father would assist him for a certain number of days when he was clearing a field or hoeing. My father got enough chickens this way to trade for a bull. Also, he accumulated rum and various herbs which Hevioso liked to drink and eat.

The service for Hevioso was in our courtyard under a canopy of grass and leaves. The thunder stone was placed on the ground by the centerpost of the canopy. When everyone had gathered in the evening, and when the drummers had arrived, my father made a water road from the spring to the centerpost. The people sang songs for Hevioso, praising him and asking for his protection. Kuku Cabrit taught them the correct songs and he enticed Hevioso along the water road with his sacred gourd rattle. That evening Hevioso entered the heads of several men and women, so that they staggered and lurched from one side to another. Hevioso was very rough with people. He rode them fiercely and threw them to the ground. When Hevioso came into my father's head he made my father run out and climb the tree that had been struck by lightning. At midnight the bull was slaughtered. Parts of the meat were cooked and offered to Hevioso on a plate set next to the thunder stone. When the service was finished, the thunder stone was brought into the house and placed in a dish and bathed with oil. In any future services for vodouns at our house Hevioso was always mentioned and implored to treat us well. Our habitation was never again struck by a thunder stone.

II

One time my mother wanted to get
some cloth to make a dress for herself and
some blouses for the boys, so she put aside
some potatoes and corn to take to the market, which was halfway down the mountain. My father wanted to have his hoe
repaired by the blacksmith, so he said he
would go along. My younger brother and I
wanted to go along, because we had never
been that far down the mountain. My
grandfather had a fever and said he would
stay behind. Besides, he said, he had already been down the mountain, in fact that
was where he had come from. So my father
took his hoe and my mother put a large
bundle of corn and potatoes on her head
and we started out before daylight. My
mother took off her sandals and put them
on top of her bundle. She said it was easier
walking on bare feet, and also she would
not wear the sandals out. My brother and I
did not have any sandals, and when we
mentioned this our father said we hadn't
lived long enough to earn them. As I was
the oldest boy I was entrusted with the difé,
a small clay pot with smoldering moss and
charcoal inside. People on long journeys al-

ways carried difé in case they might need to make a fire or light a torch.

In the early morning, heavy mist covered the trail, and white clouds filled the valleys between the mountain peaks. It was difficult to see the trail, but my father went ahead of us and felt his way with his feet. Sometimes we met other people going down to the market. The women were always carrying something to trade, and the men usually held a staff in one hand and a pot of difé in the other. After a while the mist lifted and we could see things a little better. When the sun came up we could see the Cul-de-Sac Plain and the ocean far below.

At one place we came to a fallen tree, and we sat there to rest, though my mother protested, saying that when a person carried a heavy headload she should stay on her feet because it would drain her strength and energy to sit down and get up. There was an old man already sitting there, and though we greeted him he did not reply. Several times my father spoke, but the old man did not seem to notice. My mother said that maybe he was deaf, but my father just clicked his tongue. My father offered him a small piece of bread but he ignored it. He just sat there looking across the trail, but not as if he saw anything. My father tried again to talk, saying, "Compère, is your garden up above or down below?" The old man said nothing. My father said, "I see you have a rope of banana leaves around your waist." But the old man didn't reply. After a while we got up and continued on the trail.

My mother said, "Maybe he was sick. His face didn't have any spirit in it." My father said, "No, he was under the command of a master." My brother and I said, "There was no one else there." My father answered, "Wherever he is, the master has control. He could be on the next mountain or in Gonaïves." We could not comprehend it. My father said, "The spirit was removed from the man's body by a bocor. What is left is only the living shell. The bocor keeps the man's spirit in a jar, and commands it to do whatever he wishes. The old man works in the fields or cuts wood, anything that has to be done. In the old days he was called a zombwiri. Now they say zombie. A bocor with a large plantation may have many zombies working for him." I asked my father, "Why do they stay instead of running away?" He said, "When the spirit is taken from a person's body he cannot do anything for himself, only what his master tells him to do." My mother said, "How do you know that old man back there wasn't merely dying?" My father answered, "The rope he wore around his waist was made of banana leaf fibers. That is the mark of a zombie. All zombies are tied with banana fibers."

The sun was high when we reached the market. Many women were sitting along the trail selling different kinds of things. My mother found a place and spread out her shelled corn and potatoes. My brother and I went with my father further down the trail to the house of the blacksmith, who was busy making a machete. He was an old man about my grandfather's age. He and my father had a big argument about fixing the hoe, but when they were through arguing they were very friendly. The blacksmith was a Nago, and had three scars on each cheek. He knew my grandfather and asked about him. When they were young they had been marrons together. We waited until the hoe was fixed, and my father paid him some copper coins. The blacksmith said, "Iron cuts copper," meaning that the repaired iron hoe was worth more than the payment. My father said later that blacksmiths always said that.

When we returned to the market my mother had sold most of her corn seed and potatoes and now she had some pieces of cloth, though not as much as I expected. But she had a small pig, and my brother and I took turns carrying it up the mountain when we went home. My mother said, "Before the corn grows again, this pig will be heavier than the three of you." My father said, "That pig seems to be red." He was teasing my mother, referring to a cannibal society called Red Pigs. My mother said, "Don't worry, we will eat him before he eats us."

We stopped to rest when we came to Kuku Cabrit's house, and my father told him about the old zombie. Kuku Cabrit asked if the man had a rope tied around him, and my father said yes, a rope made of banana-leaf fibers. Kuku Cabrit said, "I think there is a bocor in a valley on the other side of the mountain. I have seen several zombies recently. Be careful when you go about at night. That is when the bocor captures his zombies. People go out, they do not return. Men, women, and children. I believe I have seen this bocor. I met him on the trail. He did not molest me because he knew I have strong force within me. If you ever meet him you will recognize him. He has one brown eye and one blue eye." One of my brothers said, "If I should see him, what should I do?" Kuku Cabrit said, "If you have an egg with you, run and break the egg behind you." My brother asked, "What if I do not have an egg?" Kuku Cabrit shrugged his shoulders and smiled. "Perhaps if you are frightened enough you will lay an egg."

Later I asked my father about breaking an egg if you are pursued. He said, "Yes, there is something to it." He told us a story about an old man who wanted to be buried in a drum belonging to the elephants. "He was very sick and he said to his oldest son, whose name was Noumou, that he didn't want to be put in the earth like an ordinary person. He told his son, 'Beyond that mountain over there is a herd of elephants. Sometimes they hold vodoun services, and they play a very large drum. I want that drum for my coffin.' Noumou walked, walked, walked. He walked across the mountain. He found the herd of elephants. He hid among the trees. When it was dark, with only just a little moonlight, he waited until they were sleeping, then he went into their village and found the drum and carried it away. The elephants woke and discovered their drum had been taken. They chased Noumou. They ran very fast, and when they were catching up to him he took an egg from his knapsack and threw it on the ground behind him. Suddenly there was a large lake there, and the elephants couldn't swim. He thought he was saved. But the elephants put their trunks in the water and began to drink. They drank the lake dry and came running again. Noumou threw another egg behind him and a pine forest sprang up. The elephants struggled to get through the forest, and when they came out they chased him again. He threw down his last egg, and this time a great brush fire sprang up. Because elephants can't go through fire they had to stop and return home. So Noumou came back to his father's house with the drum. He saw his old father working in his garden. He said, 'Father, I have brought the drum.' His father answered, 'Ah, my son, that is good. But I don't need it now. I am feeling very well. Get your hoe and help me cultivate the corn.'"

I liked that story until the ending came, and I was glad to know what you could do with eggs. But I felt it was unjust that the man's son had to risk his life like that while his father wasn't really dying at all. I said, "The old man didn't even say, 'Excuse me that I made you go on that dangerous journey.'" My mother said, "The people have a saying: 'Don't complain if the funeral is cancelled, even if you are wearing your best clothes.'" After a while I said, "I have never seen any elephants in this country." My father answered, "Did I say they were in this country? Wherever they are, the story is here. Still, how can anyone be sure? Perhaps they are beyond those mountains somewhere. There are things out there we know nothing about."

One time I asked my grandfather to tell me more about using eggs to save yourself from a pursuer. He said he had heard about it, and that the story my father told me really happened back in Guinée. But he said, "Those eggs weren't just ordinary eggs, they were eggs that had been given magic powers by a practitioner of mystic science. But you can do the same thing with a wari bean, that red bean that grows wild around here. We had that bean back home, and I heard of people who used it to bar the way of an approaching enemy. They threw it on the ground and it protected them. Some people wear wari beans around their necks as protective charms. But that's not all a wari bean is good for. If you grind it up and put it in a person's food it will kill him. Before the revolution some slaves killed their masters that way. Also, it is used to turn skin from black to white. One man I knew took just a small amount of wari powder every day, and first the skin on his arms turned white, then his legs, and eventually his whole body. When he was all white he ran away from the plantation and got some shoes somewhere and said he was a Frenchman. Somebody told me this man established a plantation of his own up north and had some slaves working for him."

My grandfather was getting pretty old, and he didn't work

in the hot sun as much as before. Then one morning he didn't get up from his sleeping mat, and he told me to go down the mountain for Kuku Cabrit. Kuku Cabrit came and sat next to him and talked to him a long while, and finally he announced that my grandfather's enemy in France, the one who had made the spring stop flowing, was working against him again, but now it was more serious than the first time. My grandfather had poisoned joints—his shoulders, his knees, his fingers. Kuku Cabrit gave my mother some herbs to boil into a soup, and my grandfather had to drink it. It made him sweat a great deal, but the pain didn't go away. Kuku Cabrit said he would go back to his house and send another expedition against my grandfather's enemy. He did this, but my grandfather didn't get any better.

So Kuku Cabrit said we would have to make a big service for the vodouns and Djalan's ancestors. We prepared for one week, and my father got a bull and some white chickens for feeding the vodouns. The night of the service, Kuku Cabrit brought another houngan named Baptiste with him so that their combined knowledge would equal the power of any enemy. There were three drummers and many people came from the surrounding habitations. The houngans gave the people special songs to sing, and they made sacred cornmeal drawings on the ground. They made a water road from the spring, and different vodouns arrived and mounted people's heads.

But the vodoun Hevioso did not come, though my family had thought he was the special protector and benefactor of our household ever since the lightning bolt. The two houngans went out together and sat under a tree. They shook their rattles, calling to Hevioso. Then suddenly Baptiste was mounted by a vodoun. He talked very rapidly in a strange voice. And when they came back to the court, Kuku Cabrit said, "Papa Hevioso is not coming tonight. He is in a faraway place taking care of important matters. But he spoke through Baptiste's mouth, saying that he was sending Azaka in his place. Let us sing for Cousin Azaka, the protector of all habitants. Everyone who has a garden, Azaka will take care of him." Kuku Cabrit gave the people a special song to sing, and while they were singing he made another cornmeal drawing on the ground in honor of Azaka. He called out all of Azaka's names—Zaka, Azaka Médé, Azambra Vodoun, Azakasi Azakala, Azakala of Thunder, Azaka of the Graveyard, Minister Zaka, and Cousin Zaka. All habitants are called cousin, and because Azaka is the protector and benefactor of all cousins, he calls himself Cousin. The cornmeal drawing Kuku Cabrit made had all of Azaka's symbols in it, a garden, a machete, a long bush knife, a pipe, and a straw knapsack.

Then he went to the spring and made another water road to the dancing place. They had carried my grandfather out of the house and laid him on a mat because he could not stand up or walk. And while the drums were drumming Azaka's dance, Azaka came on the water road and went into my grandfather's head. My grandfather got up and danced, making motions with his arms as if he were cutting with his machete or long bush knife. Kuku Cabrit rushed forward and tied a kerchief around my grandfather's head, and on top of that he put a straw hat. He lighted a pipe and put it in my grandfather's mouth, and he hung a straw knapsack on his shoulder. My grandfather puffed smoke and jumped around as if he was working in his garden. After a while Kuku Cabrit and my mother took grandfather back into the house and made him lie down on his sleeping mat. Kuku Cabrit and Baptiste announced that Azaka was going to take care of him and make him well. The bull and the chickens were sacrificed and portions were set out on plates for Azaka. After more singing and dancing everyone went home.

My grandfather slept the rest of the night without waking, but in the morning he could not get up and he had pains in all his joints. Kuku Cabrit came again. All he could tell us was that some enemy vodoun appeared to be stronger than Azaka. He made Djalan sit up, and, like in the elephant story, throw eggs over his shoulder to stop any bad spirit that might be pursuing him. He gave my mother more herbs for my grandfather and then left us. My grandfather fell asleep, and after that he hardly spoke to any of us again. Sometimes he talked in his sleep but in the language of his own country. In about ten days he died.

There was a dessounin service in our house to liberate the spirit from my grandfather's head and give it freedom; if this were not done, the spirit could cause many difficulties for the family. Kuku Cabrit prayed to all the vodouns to watch over my grandfather's spirit after it had departed from his body. He said, "All you great vodouns, give hospitality to the spirit of this good man, Djalan. If he wishes to go to Yzolé Below the Water, help him. If he wishes to return to Guinée, help him, for that is where his father and mother lived. His life here on earth has been hard, but he has never done a mean thing to any living person. And even though Djalan's body was worn out, when Azaka came and rode on his shoulders, Djalan got up from his mat and danced the Cousin dance. Azaka, you especially, watch over his spirit in the world we cannot see."

Then Kuku Cabrit kneeled astride Djalan's corpse and spoke to him. He said, "Djalan, my old friend, you decided to leave us at last. We will miss you. We will cry, but we will console ourselves because we will remember you and you will remember us. Now is the moment when your vodoun will leave your head and go its own way. Therefore I say to you, Djalan, sit up. Wake up this last time, Djalan, and sit up. Djalan, sit up, sit up, sit up. I call on your protector, Azaka, to help you. Azaka, vodoun of the mountain gardens, help Djalan sit up so that his spirit may be freed. Sit up, Djalan, sit up!"

Djalan's body trembled a little, then sat up. His eyes opened and he looked into Kuku Cabrit's eyes. Kuku Cabrit shook his rattle, and he touched Djalan's forehead with a small earthen jar. He said, "Everything is done now, Djalan. Lie down and sleep." Djalan's eyes closed and he lay down. Kuku Cabrit put a cover on the jar. He said, "Djalan, your spirit is now in this jar. We will set it free." He went to the door of the house and threw the jar on the earth, shattering it. The spirit of my grandfather was liberated. I do not know where it went, though I believe it returned to his home in Guinée. Kuku Cabrit said to my father and mother, "Do not cry too much. He will be present all the time. Sometimes you may hear his voice coming from the spring."

After we buried my grandfather we set out a constant guard at the grave, so that some malevolent bocor would not dig the body up and make my grandfather a zombie slave. Kuku Cabrit advised it because he thought the bocor with one brown and one blue eye might be in our part of the mountains, and we had all heard of zombies being sighted here and there. One person from the city told of having buried his brother and then seeing him again in the streets of the city wearing a girdle of banana fiber rope. He went to his brother to talk to him, but his brother didn't recognize him at all. So for ten nights different members of our family sat by my grandfather's grave to make sure it wasn't disturbed. I myself spent three nights there without sleeping, holding a sharp machete in my hand in case of trouble. After ten nights it wasn't necessary any more.

As the old people explained it to me, there were several ways a bocor could take a person and make him into zombie. One was to take a corpse from a fresh grave, make a magic ceremony and cause the body to become alive. If the person had had his spirit liberated before being buried, then the bocor simply instructed him to do this or that and he would do it, because he had no inner force of his own. But if for some reason the person hadn't had his spirit liberated, then he might resist the bocor's commands. He might refuse to come out of the grave, and the bocor would go away and let him remain there. Sometimes a bocor would administer a poison drug to a person and that person would appear to die. After burial the bocor would come after him in the night and give him another drug to bring his body back to life again, and he would do whatever the bocor ordered him to do. Sometimes a knife was pressed into the heart of a corpse before burial so that the body would not be useful to a bocor. There were so many things to know about a proper and safe burial that a family almost always went to a houngan to find out what to do. I mention these things about zombies because a little later on in my life I came to be involved with them without wishing to do so.

III

I was a grown man by the time a vodoun first mounted and rode me. How it happened was this. We were attending a First Yam service at Kuku Cabrit's, and he was calling on this vodoun and that vodoun to come from Yzolé Below the Water to accept a share of the first yams. He was signalling with his rattle to guide the vodouns to the center of the dance court, where plates of food had been set out for them. I was just standing to one side, singing with the others, when I saw a bright flash of light and felt a great weight on my shoulders. I fell to the ground, got up, and lurched one way and another. I did not feel any more like Dosu Bordeaux, but as if I were some other person. I seemed to be fighting in a battle with my long double machete in my hands. Kuku Cabrit handed me a bottle of rum, and after I drank from it I went around pouring rum into people's mouths. Kuku Cabrit put gunpowder on my tongue and I washed it down with rum. I cannot remember everything I did, but I know that after a while I felt very weak and fell on the ground. People took me inside Kuku Cabrit's house and I instantly went to sleep.

When I woke up, Kuku Cabrit was

there shaking his rattle over me and singing a song to Ogoun. He told me that Ogoun had claimed me, and would come again whenever he wished to enter my head and ride me. He told me Ogoun was a very fiery vodoun who could be very rough with his horses, but he had great force in the universe and could do good things for me and my family. After that night whenever I heard drums playing an Ogoun salute or people singing to Ogoun I would feel my body tingling in a strange way, but only once in a while did Ogoun enter my head, usually at a special service of some kind. I knew when he was coming because my head would become very uneasy as if it were being made ready. Whenever it happened at Kuku Cabrit's services, he would put a jacket with epaulets, like a general's, on me and put a saber in my hand. Kuku Cabrit told me I would never die of poisoning, because Ogoun protected his people from that.

Ogoun belonged to the Nago nation, and because Kuku Cabrit was a Nago he was very pleased that Ogoun had chosen me to be one of his people. Where he lived in Guinée, Ogoun was the vodoun of iron and master of all blacksmiths. It was he, Kuku Cabrit said, who had brought to the people the knowledge of making iron. Before Ogoun came everyone made tools out of copper, so their bush knives and hoes were not very strong. Their tools easily bent and became dull, so the people could not work very long in their gardens. They had to go home and sharpen everything. After Ogoun showed them how to make iron tools they accomplished much more. Because spears and knives and guns came to be made of iron, Ogoun was also the vodoun of war. That is why Kuku Cabrit put a saber in my hand when Ogoun mounted into my head. To show that Ogoun was my protector and my mother's, I made a small shrine to him in front of our house by the door. It consisted of small pieces of iron that I gathered, pieces of broken iron pots and hoes. So our house had three protective spirits, Hevioso, Ogoun, and Azaka, and whenever we had a service we called on them before the others. Some people did not have any protective spirits, and they were considered unfortunate.

My younger brother was named Jean-Jacques. My parents called him that after General Jean-Jacques Dessalines who drove the French out of Haiti. Jean-Jacques married a grand-daughter of Kuku Cabrit and built his own house a little distance from ours, higher on the mountain. It took him quite a while to clear out the trees and brush near his house so he could have his own garden. My father and I helped him with his work, so he was obligated to come back from time to time to work on my father's land. Some other habitants also helped him, and in return he had to help them with their work when they needed him. Those habitants who exchanged work with my brother called their group Habitation of the Beautiful Pines, and they had a flag of their own which they carried wherever they were working.

Sometimes the work was quite hard, like when a field had to be cleared of trees, but there was pleasure in it as well as fatigue. Often there was a drummer, and he was accompanied by somebody who beat a stone against a hoe blade, and the men made up songs to sing so that they would work rhythmically. They had a saying that one hoe falling by itself cannot make music. So the drum set the beat and all the hoes would go up and down together, or if they were cutting trees all the axes would strike wood at the same time. Sometimes a man would make up a song about a beautiful girl he had been with down in a banana grove, and how he had taught her something to remember. Occasionally there would be a song about the zeaubeaups who lived in a certain mapou tree and who came out at night to find people to eat.

If a certain member didn't come to help someone when he was needed he was expelled from the society and no one would go to his place when he was doing his own heavy labor. When the men were working they might make up a song about such a person. One song I remember was about a man named François who always seemed to be sick whenever the society gathered to work on someone's land. It went: "Oh, where is our friend François? Where is our friend François? François has the colic, he has a broken leg today. François has a fever, he has a sore behind today. Oh, where is François?" Nobody liked to have a song like that sung about him. Once it was sung it might be heard again and again at different Saturday night dances. In the evening after the work was done, the family whose land was being worked would feed everyone generously, and later there would be a good-time dance outside the house. Several times when my brother couldn't attend a work party he asked me to go in his place. The eating and dancing were very enjoyable. I met new girls, and sometimes I was able to arrange a rendezvous with a girl I liked. But we had to be careful, because if someone found out about it the girl might have a song made up about her.

The first child my brother and his wife had was a boy. He seemed to have a strong body, but a bad coughing sickness overtook him and he died before he was a year old. People said that because he died so young his spirit went back to a certain place under the water and waited with other babies to be born again. Kuku Cabrit told my brother a baby who died young like that was called an abiku. Some abikus were born, died, and born again many times. My brother's second child was also a boy and looked very much like the first one. Kuku Cabrit made a divining service and learned that the second child was really the same one who had come before. My brother and his wife were very happy to have the first one return after they thought they had lost him forever, and they gave him the name Thank You Small One for Coming Back, but it was too long a name to carry around, and some children made fun of it, so in time it became just Merci Pitit, Thank You Small One.

IV

One year the society Jean-Jacques belonged to did not have enough seed at
planting time, and they delegated my
brother and another man, André LaFitte, to
go down the mountain to a village called
Dleau Frète to find some. My mother gave
Jean-Jacques a chicken to take with him to
trade for some cloth. My brother and André
started out early in the morning while the
trail was still covered with mist. They carried a pot of embers with them in case they
might have to stop in the woods somewhere
and make a fire. The mountain nights were
quite cold. We thought they would be back
in two or three days, but by the fourth day
we had not yet seen them. Two men from
the Habitation of the Beautiful Pines came
to our house and asked us if Jean-Jacques
and André had passed along our trail, and
we said no, they must have taken a different
trail. The men said the two of them had not
arrived. On the fifth day and the sixth day
my brother and André still were not seen by
anyone. They did not return at all.

After fourteen days the men of the society went to a diviner named Conrolé who
lived over the crest of our mountain. Conrolé consulted all of his divining things, his

knotted cords, his Ifa seeds, and his wari tray. He told the men that Jean-Jacques and André had gone into the mist and been overtaken by some evil event, but he could not tell them any more than that. My father and I went to see Kuku Cabrit, who divined with his sliding shell and other things, but he was unable to find out anything. He said, "Are they alive? Are they dead? We do not know. Perhaps the ancestors can tell us."

He took up his ritual rattle and a little bell, and he began to shake them and sing in a very low voice. He sang on and on, and I thought after a while that he was only wasting time. Then suddenly his body stiffened and his eyes rolled back. Gurgling sounds came out of his mouth and spittle ran down his chin. The gurgling sounds became a faint familiar voice. I heard my grandfather Djalan speaking as if he were far away and very tired. I heard him say, "Yes, yes, I am here. Why are you disturbing my rest?" Kuku Cabrit replied in his own voice, "Pardon me, Djalan, my friend, this is Kuku Cabrit speaking to you." And my grandfather answered irritably, "Yes, I know who you are. What do you want?" Kuku Cabrit said, "My good friend, your family misses you. We would not bother you but we have to know something. Your grandson Jean-Jacques and André LaFitte have disappeared, and we need to know if they have joined you down there below the water." From Kuku Cabrit's mouth we heard my grandfather say, "Ah, that boy, he is always doing something to upset people. No, he is not down here. He and André LaFitte are still living up there somewhere. Tell the family not to forget me, Djalan, the Bambara. Tell them to put food on my grave when they celebrate the yam harvest." Kuku Cabrit answered, "Yes, Djalan, my friend. They will remember you."

Kuku Cabrit stopped shaking his rattle and fell backward on the floor where he was sitting. No more voices came from his mouth, either his own or my grandfather's. He lay silently for a while as if he were sleeping. When at last he sat up, sweat was running down his face. He wiped his face with his head cloth. He said, "Djalan has told us that Jean-Jacques and André are not there, so they must still be alive. I cannot tell you any more. If Jean-Jacques and André do not come back soon someone will have to go looking for them." My father and I went home. We told everyone what Kuku Cabrit had divined.

We waited day after day, often looking down the trail that descended our mountain. We asked travelers coming our way if they had seen Jean-Jacques or André, but there was no news of them. So one morning my father dressed in his best denim shirt, put some food in his knapsack, and started out for Dleau Frète. In a short while he came back to get his cocomacaque stick so that he would have protection against any bakas or other demons if he should meet them on the way. Then he left again.

In three days he returned from Dleau Frète. He reported that he had gone through the village asking people if they had seen my brother and André. One old woman said she saw them going toward the habitation of a man named Justin, who had seed to trade, so my father went there but Justin told him that Jean-Jacques and André never arrived at his house. My father asked where they might have gone if they never arrived, and Justin said, "Can anyone tell? There are no habitations between here and the village." Going back again to the village my father looked for other trails but did not find any.

After he returned home we went on expecting that Jean-Jacques would appear one evening and tell a long story about where he had been, but in time it became clear to us that he was not coming. One day Jean-Jacques' wife came to see us with her child, Merci Pitit. While my mother was playing with him Merci Pitit said, "Where is my papa?" Then we all became quiet, until my father said, "We cannot leave it this way. Someone will have to search for Jean-Jacques."

That night I had strange dreams about my brother. I was somewhere, though I don't know where it was, and I seemed to hear Jean-Jacques calling from a grove of trees. The brush was very dense and I had to cut my way through with my machete. I came to a clearing where there was a house and a garden. I saw Jean-Jacques standing in the middle of the clearing, but I don't know how I recognized him because his head was gone from his shoulders. He was carrying his head in his arms, and the head was talking. All it said was, "Dosu, Dosu."

A man came out of the house with a long whip in his hand, and he was cracking the whip and shouting at Jean-Jacques. Jean-Jacques dropped his head on the ground and let it roll down the mountainside, and the man chased it, shouting for it to stop.

In the morning when I woke up I told my father and mother that I was the one to go find my brother because Jean-Jacques was calling me. My father argued at first, saying it was too much for me. I said Jean-Jacques had called me in my sleep. He said, "Where will you begin?" I said, "I will begin. I will take the first step and the second step. I will go where the vodouns guide me. If I take a false turn I will come back and try another turn." At last my father agreed. He gave me his best machete and the scabbard he had made for it. My mother put bread in my knapsack, and she also gave me some small coins she had been saving in a rag stuffed into the wall. I left early in the morning.

I stopped at Kuku Cabrit's habitation to tell him where I was going. I said I would go to Dleau Frète first, and after that wherever the trail might lead. I said, "Since he is not dead he is somewhere." I told him about my dream the previous night and he looked very solemn. He questioned me and said, "The dream tells us Jean-Jacques is in distress, but it says nothing about where he is. Perhaps he is on a distant mountain. How will you know which direction to take?" I said I did not know. Kuku Cabrit said, "The dream seems to say some person or evil force has taken possession of Jean-Jacques' mind and he is helpless. It could be a baka or a bocor who is enslaving him, or even a vodoun. Perhaps your grandfather's old enemy has sent an expedition against him. Perhaps his head-spirit has been stolen from his head. Even if you find him how will you deal with such a thing?" I said I did not know.

Kuku Cabrit made me come into his house and sit down. He began to gather objects together for me. First he gave me a small medicine packet to hang around my neck to help protect my body from harm. Then he gave me a small fragment of iron to put in my pocket, a talisman to remind the vodoun Ogoun that I was one of his children. He gave me some colored beads to wear to protect me from illness. He gave me a short cocomacaque stick to carry in case I should be molested by a baka. He gave me a short knotted divining cord to help me find my way if I should become lost. And he took some indigo and marked small figures meaning crossroads on my arms.

He said, "For anyone on a long journey like yours, Legba, the spirit of the highway, is the most important vodoun of all. Remember that any crossroad is a very dangerous place. It is there that the force of Legba is strongest. From the crossroad, every direction but one is wrong. Legba can help you or hinder you. If he feels like it he will send you the wrong way and perhaps you will never be able to return. If you come to a crossroad and your direction is not clear to you, make his sign in the dust and call his name. You can call him Legba, Attibon, Eshu, or Master of the Highway. I will give you a song to placate him." And Kuku Cabrit gave me the song:

Attibon Legba, my vodoun, open the way for me.
Master of the Highway, let me pass safely by

He also gave me some mystical words to pronounce after the song: "Agoé! Agola! Agochi!"

I thanked Kuku Cabrit for everything, but I told him I did not have anything to offer him in return for his help. He said, "I do not want anything. Jean-Jacques is the husband of my granddaughter. Your grandfather Djalan was my good friend. What I have given you, a cow and a hundred chickens could not pay for it. Your safety is what I care about. Make your journey. Find Jean-Jacques if you can and return home."

V

This was the way my search for my brother began. I will tell everything just the way it happened. Believe or do not believe, I cannot help it. There is more to the world, visible and invisible, than I ever imagined. We know that the vodouns are here, or in Guinée, or under the water even if we are not aware of them until they come into a person's head. And we know that the ancestors reside somewhere even if they do not often speak to us. Bondieu, the sky god, who is greater than all things in the world, is invisible but is he not there all the time? You cannot see a baka unless he wishes to be seen, and a lougaro looks like an ordinary person until he goes out into the night to do whatever evil thing is in his mind. Most of the world is not seen at all except when it wants to be seen. We cannot be certain about anything. This is what I learned on my journey while searching for my brother.

I continued walking until I came to Dleau Frète. At the place where the women sat along the road to sell their garden produce I asked questions, but no one really remembered Jean-Jacques or André. Only one old woman seemed to recall something. She said, "Some time ago a man came here asking the same question. I told him I saw them going to Justin's habitation." I said, "Yes, it was my father. He went to see Justin, but Justin said they never arrived at his place." The old woman said, "Then who knows where they went? Maybe they went to the city down below." I told the woman we had reasons to think they had not gone that way. She looked closely at me. She lighted her clay pipe. Then she asked, "Reasons? What reasons?" I remembered the saying, "Know much, tell little." So I said only that we had consulted a diviner. She turned away to sell some coffee beans to another woman.

When she was finished she said to me, "Behind the mountains are mountains. Behind one diviner is another. Come to my house over there by the cashew tree this evening." I did not understand why I should go to her house, but I stayed in Dleau Frète and found a place to lie down to rest. I slept, but I was awakened by a goat chewing on my straw knapsack. I chased him away and then walked here and there in the village. I asked a girl, "Where is the trail to Justin's habitation?" She waved her hand toward the mountainside. Up above I saw a small lime-plastered house and a man working in a steep garden.

In the evening I ate a piece of bread and after that I went to the house by the cashew tree. The old woman and a young girl were pestling grain. The old woman did not greet me. She said, "Here, take my pestle and pestle for me." I did not want to do it, because pestling was a woman's housework. But I took the pestle and the young girl and I worked together. After a while the old woman called me to come into the house and motioned for me to sit on a mat. She asked if I knew her name, and I said no, I had not heard anyone mention it. She said her name was Délina Lafleur, and that she knew my name was Dosu. I asked how she knew it and she said she had the power to know.

She said, "Did you bring anything to pay me?" I told her I didn't have anything to bring. She asked, "What about the money your mother gave you?" I said, "It is very small money, no more than fifty cob." She said, "It is seventy cob." I took out the coins and counted them. There were seventy cob. I said, "Mama, you have the gift of sight." She said, "Half for you and half for me." I put the coins in her hand. She closed her eyes and sang some words I did not understand. Then she told me, "Go up Justin's trail, but not all the way. You will see a strip of white cloth tied to the branch of a small pine. Turn there and walk toward the next mountain." I asked if there was a path, and she said, "Yes, but it is invisible." I said, "Mama, if there is a path how can it be invisible?" She answered, "Because those who use it do not have any physical substance, therefore they leave no footprints." I slept in the old woman's house and left before sunrise.

I went up the trail toward Justin's habitation and found the tree with the strip of white cloth. I did not find any path leading from Justin's trail, and I could not decide whether to do what the old woman had instructed me to do. The heavy morning mist still clung to the mountain and I told myself I should wait until the mist lifted. When the air was beginning to clear I saw that the way I was supposed to go led into a deep gully with a steep hill on the other side. No habitations were visible, even though I heard voices coming from that direction. I thought I should appeal to the Master of the Highway before doing anything else, so I made Legba's sign in the dust and sang the song Kuku Cabrit had given me.

At that moment I saw a ragged old man coming up Justin's trail. He was crippled, and one of his legs was twined around a crotch-cane so that he seemed to have one good leg and one wooden leg. I greeted him respectfully. He smiled at me and I saw that he had no teeth. When he arrived where I was standing he placed his wooden leg in the center of the Legba sign I had drawn and spun around on it, all the while grinning and showing his toothless gums. The heavy mist wafted back for a moment, and when it lifted, the old man was not there any more. He was not on the trail and he was not down in the gully. No ordinary person could disappear like that, surely not a crippled old man. I thought that perhaps I had seen a baka, but then I remembered that Legba the Master of the Highway always appeared in our vodoun ceremonies as an old man with a crotch-cane. It came to my mind then that the person I had just seen probably was Legba himself.

He had not spoken to me but he had smiled, and that seemed a good sign. Yet he hadn't indicated whether the route I was about to take was a good one or a bad one. Nevertheless, I turned off Justin's trail and descended into the gully. I heard goats and cows as I went down, but I did not see them or any cattle droppings. When I reached the bottom I saw a garden down there. I heard hoes chopping on the earth but didn't see any habitants. There were voices all around me, just as if I were in Dleau Frète, but I saw no people. A dog barked nearby, but I couldn't see him. I looked for someone to ask whether Jean-Jacques and André had been there. Finally I called out, "Has anyone seen my brother and his friend?" The voices stopped for a moment and I heard someone answer, "Not here, not here. Pass on, wherever you are going."

I crossed the gully as quickly as I could, wondering what kind of spirits or demons were living there. Kuku Cabrit had never mentioned them, and Délina Lafleur had only hinted about creatures with no physical substance. I was glad that they hadn't hurt me, but felt anxious to get out of that place. On the far side of the gully I began to climb toward the crest. There were no signs of people anywhere. No trees had been cut, no ground had been tilled. There were many loose stones, and once I slipped and cut my foot. I tore a strip from my shirt to bind the cut, and after that I had to climb more slowly, but by the middle of the day I had reached the top, from where I could see more mountains beyond.

I sat down to rest and pondered why I was going in this direction into the wilderness. It was only because the old woman Délina Lafleur told me to do it. But who was Délina Lafleur? Perhaps she herself was some kind of baka or a human malefactor. Perhaps she had even sent Jean-Jacques and André to this same place. I was sitting very still, and a small zandolite lizard climbed up on my bandaged foot. The two of us looked into each other's eyes, not moving. I began to wonder if he was asking me a question. He was watching me so intently that I felt I should say something.

Slowly, so as not to startle him, I reached into my knapsack and brought out the piece of iron Kuku Cabrit had given me as a sign I was under the protection of Ogoun. I held it up for him to see. He moved his head up and down several times and extended his throat. I also pulled out the medicine packet from under my shirt and held it up. Again he moved his head up and down, then scampered into the underbrush. I wondered if I had been stupid, showing these things to a lizard, but at least no harm had come of it.

Now that I was on the top of the mountain I had no idea what to do or where to go. There were no habitations, and except for the pine forest all around me the country was desolate. I looked one way and then another for some kind of a sign. I thought, "Ah, Legba, you spirit of the road! You were there on Justin's trail. You grinned at me and let me go down into the gully, just as Délina Lafleur instructed me to do, knowing all the time I would merely end up in the wilderness." But I thought about the zandolite lizard. He had gone toward the west. Perhaps that was a sign.

So at last I got up and walked westward, slowly because of my injured foot, making my way through the brush and trees as if I really knew where I was going. Sometimes I had to use my machete to clear my way among the vines. When the sun was beginning to go down I found myself in country with fewer trees. I saw a faint trail on the ground and followed it. I heard voices ahead and supposed that they came from a village or at least from a homestead of a few houses. The light was dimming but I went forward, expecting to see people before long.

The first living creatures I saw were two large boars coming in my direction as if to meet me. They appeared to be wild and unfriendly, so I halted and took my machete from its scabbard. When the boars were very close, they also stopped. Although I was nervous, I found myself laughing, because the boars seemed to be wearing French shoes on their back feet and French gloves on their front feet. I wondered if they were going to dance the Calinda. Then one of them said, "Your machete is no good against us. We belong to the Red Pig Society." I put the machete away and took hold of my cocomacaque stick. The other boar said, "Your cocomacaque is no good either, because you are standing on terrain that belongs to our society."

I said, "Messieurs, I am sorry. I didn't know I was on your terrain." They said, "Sorry is not enough. Now you are here. Our people are hungry, and you will have to come with us." I realized that neither my father nor Kuku Cabrit had told me enough about how to deal with Red Pigs. But I tried to make conversation. I said, "Messieurs, are you French Red Pigs or Haitian Red Pigs?" They said, "French Red Pigs. But what does it matter to you?" I thought of the saying, "Because a man wears French shoes doesn't make him a plantation owner." They said, "We heard what you were thinking." I said, "If you are French this land is not yours. The Revolution is over. You belong in France." They said to each other, "If he will not come, we will have to take him by force."

I did not wait for them to do that. I turned and ran back the way I had come as fast as I could on my wounded foot. I heard them following me making wild boar sounds and they seemed to be getting closer. Suddenly I remembered my garde corps, the medicine packet Kuku Cabrit had given me to wear around my neck. I took it off and turned around, holding it in front of me. The two Red Pigs veered off the trail and went running in a different direction. Soon I could not hear them any more.

I said to myself, "Thank you, Kuku Cabrit, for the garde corps you gave me." I thought of Délina Lafleur who had told me to go to this place. I said to myself, "Mama Délina, a day will come when you will regret it." I also thought of Legba At-tibon, the toothless old vodoun who did not prevent me from going into this wilderness. I reproached him out loud, saying, "Master of the Highway, what did I ever do to you that you should treat me like this? I respect you, my family respects you. We have danced for you and given you a feast. Oh misery! Why do you punish me this way?" Even though it was already night, I marked Legba's sign on the earth and sang a song to impor-tune him:

Attibon, my Attibon, open the way for me.
Attibon Legba, open the way for me to pass.

It was too dark for me to see anything, so I found my way to the nearest tree. I sat on the ground and leaned against the trunk. I did not sleep because the night air was too cold. I remembered my mother saying, "The fortunate man sits by his fire, but the man without a blanket shivers to keep warm."

When the moon rose I was able to see. It was a bright moon, and I thought I ought to keep going. The sooner I was beyond this mountain the better it would be for me. The stars showed me that I was going north. As I passed a certain tree I heard a young woman's voice coming from it, saying, "Come in, join me here inside the tree. My body is warm." I hurried on. Occasionally I heard voices from other trees, some offering me water to drink or food to eat. Though I was very tired I did not want to stop where the trees were talking. It was a dangerous place.

I went on in the night. And after a great deal of walking I saw lights in the distance. As they came closer, I could see a procession of men and women, or at least I then thought them to be men and women, carrying pine torches. In the front of the procession a man carried a flag, and following him four men were carrying a body lashed to a plank. It was clearly a funeral, though I had never heard of a funeral in the middle of the night, so I moved to one side to let the procession pass. But when it arrived near where I was standing it stopped and everyone turned to look at me. I was frightened by the sight of their faces, which seemed fleshless. I could not see eyes, only skull sockets. They did not speak, but I felt they were condemning me for being there while the funeral was passing.

I felt compelled to say something. I said, "Messieurs, Mesdames, excuse me, I didn't know you were coming this way. I am sorry someone has died." The man who carried the flag answered, "You who wear living flesh, who are you?" I said I was Dosu Bordeaux on a journey. He said, "Aaah, now we must have two funerals." I said, "But you are carrying only one corpse." He replied, "No, he is not a corpse, he is living. That is why we are burying him." I said, "I do not understand why you would bury someone who is living. That would be against the wishes of God in the Sky." He became angry and said roughly,

"All of you who have flesh on your bones have no understanding. We are the Dry Bone People. Once we were buried, but a great bocor brought us out of our graves. Though we were no longer alive, the great bocor restored movement to our bodies. He gave us a village. He said, 'Here you are to stay. If any of you ever becomes alive, bury him with all respect.' This man on the plank became alive. Therefore we performed all the ceremonies and now we are about to put him into the ground." I looked at the man on the plank. He called to me weakly, "Save me, save me."

I did not know how to save him. The man with the flag said to me, "Wait here. We will come back for you." The funeral procession moved on. I watched the torches grow smaller in the night. Then I began running. I did not know where I was going, but I ran till I fell from exhaustion. I did not cry aloud, but I abused Legba in my thoughts. I said, "You, Legba, have put a curse on me. Therefore I curse you. May you dry up like the Dry Bone People. May your wooden crotch-cane be eaten by ants and beetles."

There was a flash of blue light in front of my eyes and an unbearable weight on my shoulders. I felt Legba entering my head. Then I was on my feet dancing and whirling. My leg was twined around Legba's crotch-cane, and I spun around on it like a top. Words came out of my mouth, but I did not know what they were. Suddenly the moon and stars went out of the sky, and I sank down in blackness. I heard nothing and saw nothing.

VI

It seemed as if only a moment had passed when I opened my eyes and found myself lying on a mat in a house. Daylight flooded through the open door. Thinking of the frightening events of the night, I did not try to get up until a woman came in bringing me a cup of coffee. A few moments later a bearded man entered. He said, "Ah, you are awake." After looking at me a while he asked, "Where do you come from?" I said in the country above Dleau Frète. He asked what I was doing out there in the night, and I said I was making a journey. He said, "It was fortunate for you that I came along when I did. It is bad country." I said, yes, very bad. He said, "If I were not a bocor you would still be there. There was a loa in your head and he did not want to go away." I said, "A loa?" He said, "Yes, a vodoun. Here we call them loa. I importuned him to leave you. I made a small service for you, then he went away." I said, "It was the Master of the Highway." He said, "Legba was very angry with you. He wanted you to dash yourself to pieces." I said, "I rebuked him for sending me on a false trail." He replied, "That is what Legba will do unless you placate him. He makes people do wild and improper things. He is a hard loa."

He took out a divining board and threw shells on it and studied them. After pondering a while he said, "I know your name, Dosu Bordeaux." I acknowledged it, and he said, "I see from the shells that you are searching for someone." I told him about Jean-Jacques and André. He clicked his tongue. "Ah, but what brought you here?" I said I did not know, I merely followed signs, and Legba allowed me to come this way. He said, "Don't you have any personal guardian spirits?" I said yes, Ogoun. He said that if I had called on Ogoun the previous night he might have interceded with Legba for me. I said, "I did not know it."

He put his divining board away. He asked, "Do you know who I am?" I answered, "No, M'sieu', please excuse me for that." He said, "I am called Bocor Zandolite." I said, "Is it you? I once heard about a great houngan named Bocor Zandolite. During the day he had the form of a zandolite, but at night he took on human form." He nodded but did not say anything. I said, "At a certain place a zandolite sat on my foot, then he went to the west and I followed him." He nodded again but did not speak. Though he did not say yes or no to anything, I knew it was he who had guided me. He was a very powerful bocor. It was said that Bocor Zandolite had great authority and influence with the vodouns.

Bocor Zandolite's wife tended my wounded foot for me. She made a lotion out of roots, bathed the wound, and wrapped my foot in a red cloth. Later, Bocor Zandolite questioned me. He said, "You are searching for your brother, but do you know where you are going? No, you are merely wandering in dangerous country. Why do you believe you will be able to find your brother without a map? Why do you think he is somewhere in these mountains and not at Cap Haïtien?" I said I did not know. He said, "You are inexperienced, like a child." I answered respectfully, "Yes, Papa." He said, "I would help you, but nothing is free. What do you have that you can give me as payment?" I said I had nothing, only a few copper coins. He asked, "Are you willing to undertake an engagement?" I said I did not understand what an engagement was. He said, "You make a promise to perform some action for me when I want it. It is not an ordinary promise. If you do not fulfill it when the time comes, unfortunate things will happen to you. The flesh on your legs will melt away and you will become a dry bone person." I said, "Papa, if you can help me find my brother I will make an engagement with you." Bocor Zandolite said, "Good, then I will see what I can do."

He sat on a low stool and I sat on the ground facing him. He placed a small earthen jar to my mouth and told me to repeat these words into it: "I, Dosu Bordeaux, pledge in the name of all the spirits of Guinée, in the name of all the Creole spirits, in the name of the King of the Sky, in the name of all our ancestors, in the name of the vodouns of the air, the land and the sea, that I will keep my engagement with Bocor Zandolite. I will do whatever the loa Pinga Maza requires when the time comes, or I will suffer the penalty assigned to me." When I had spoken the words into the jar, he quickly put a stopper in it, saying, "Now you are bound to Pinga Maza. The jar will be buried in the earth, and the compact will be alive wherever you may be. The day you pay your debt the jar will break of its own accord and the engagement will be finished."

Then Bocor Zandolite took up his beaded rattle and recited a long invocation to Pinga Maza. Soon his body started to tremble and jerk, because Pinga Maza was taking possession of him. He picked up a bottle, shattered it against a stone, and began to eat broken glass, which is Pinga Maza's food. Several times I heard him mention my name, and also my brother's name and André Lafitte's. I expected to see blood on his lips from the broken glass, but there was nothing. I wondered how long he could live with the glass in his stomach, but I suppose his vodoun protected him from harm. When Pinga Maza went out of his body, Bocor Zandolite became limp. He stopped shaking his rattle and his chin sank down on his chest. Suddenly another vodoun mounted him and he picked up a pen and a small piece of sheepskin on which he commenced to draw mystic figures. He drew until the sheepskin was full of marks, after which his possession left him and he became still.

He seemed very tired. When he had rested a while he said, "Here, Dosu Bordeaux, is your passport. If at any time you do not know what to do next or where to go, consult the passport. It will be your map. Sleep here tonight, and tomorrow morning resume your journey. Protect the passport. Do not lose it." I accepted the sheepskin and examined it. I said, "Papa, I cannot read what it says." He answered, "The writings are made by the spirit Congo Mapiongle. Find a bocor of the Loango nation who can read these signs, then you will know what is written. Meanwhile, carry the passport wherever you go and it will protect you from dangers."

I said, "Papa Zandolite, thank you for placating Legba when he was tormenting me. Thank you also for your divination. But I need to know about my brother Jean-Jacques and his friend André. Where are they? Is my brother in danger? Is he sick or wounded? What shall I do to put myself on the right trail?"

Bocor Zandolite said, "Take the western trail, I can't tell you anything more. Now follow me." We went together to the back of his house. He dug a deep hole there and buried the jar into which I had spoken my engagement. He said, "Do not forget. When I need you I will let you know."

I stayed in Bocor Zandolite's house that night, and the next morning I took the trail he had indicated. It crossed the ridge of the mountain, then descended. I saw many other mountains beyond and wondered how many of them I would have to cross to find out what had happened to Jean-Jacques. I walked all day, and finally, down below, I found a river. On the other side was a clearing and a small lime plastered house. I thought, "Perhaps here is a Loango bocor." I forded at a shallow place and approached the house.

Nearby I saw a man tending a garden. He was strangely dressed in a long black robe and I could see that the skin of his face was white. I hesitated, because he was the first white man I had ever seen. But he waved to me, saying, "Welcome, young friend, do not be afraid. This is a place of God." A cross hung from a chain around his neck, and I thought, "Ah, the sign of Legba of the Highway." I thought I should turn away, because Legba did not like me, but the man kept calling me.

Before going any further I made Legba's sign on the ground and sang the song Kuku Cabrit had taught me, after which I spoke the mystic words, "Agoé! Agola! Agochi!" The man came forward and took me by the hand. He said, "My son, I can see that you are a weary traveler. Come to my house and rest." We went into the house, where he sat me at a table and gave me a gourd of akasan, though he would not let me eat until he put his hands together and invoked the vodoun Jesus. He asked me many questions, and I explained to him that I was searching for my brother and André. He said we should pray to Jesus for guidance, and he took me into a room with a large cross painted on the wall, in front of which was a small table. The room looked something like the inner room at Kuku Cabrit's, but there were no divining trays or thunder stones or clay jars containing head-spirits of the dead. He got down on his knees and put his hands together and called on his vodoun to assist me. He made me kneel also, and I said the mystic words, "Agoé! Agola! Agochi!"

Afterwards he asked me if I was a follower of Satan, and I said I didn't know anything about Satan, but that I had been mounted by both Ogoun and Legba, and that Ogoun was my protector. He asked me to repeat the words I had said while he was invoking his spirit, and I said, "Agoé, Agola, Agochi." He said, "My son, those are devilish words. Wipe them from your mind and soul. I will give you good new words to replace them. Say after me, 'Father, Son and Holy Spirit.'" I said the words and he was pleased with me. I asked him if his guardian spirit was as strong as Ogoun. He smiled and said, "He is the strongest in the world. It is Father God and all his saints who control our lives." I asked him if there were many saints, and he said, "Yes, many, many." I said, "Just like our vodouns."

I showed him the passport that Bocor Zandolite had given me, saying it had come from the vodoun Congo Mapiongle. I wanted to know if he could read the signs on it. He said, "Ah, my son, these are writings of Satan! Let us burn them!" And before I could prevent him he threw my passport into the fire. I became angry. I said that to get this passport I had to make an engagement with a powerful bocor, and that my pledge was in a jar buried in the ground, so I had made the compact for nothing. He said, "No, no, my son, you do not understand. You have purified yourself, and for what you have done Jesus will look on you with favor. Here, take this and wear it around your neck. It will protect you from all kinds of dangers." It was a cross similar to the one he himself was wearing, but much smaller. I accepted it and put it in my pocket.

I asked him if Jesus could tell me where to find my brother. He said he would pray for me that Jesus would give me guidance, and I was to do the same. "Have faith in Jesus," he said, "and he will reveal himself to you." I was very glad I had not showed him the medicine packet under my shirt and the piece of Ogoun's iron in my knapsack, for I am sure he would have taken them and destroyed them. I wanted to leave his house, but I looked at the mountain I had to climb and it seemed very high, so when he invited me to stay until morning I accepted. He said, "Now let us go and do God's work in the field," and we went out to his garden and hoed. We did not stop until darkness began to fall, then we went back to the house. He gave me more akasan, but he would not let me eat it until he had gotten on his knees and recited a service to his vodoun. He gave me a mat to sleep on, and that night I had frightening dreams. I dreamed that the white bocor in the black cloak was dancing with one leg around Legba's crotch-cane, and I also dreamed that I was inside a great hollow mapou tree with a crowd of dancing Red Pigs. When I awoke I was glad. The white bocor gave me a cup of coffee with sugar, but before I left he made me recite five times, "Father, Son and Holy Spirit." As soon as I was a little distance from the house I said, "Agoé! Agola! Agochi!" And I asked Ogoun to guide me away from any more white bocors.

I was beginning to feel weak from hunger because I had not had much to eat since leaving Dleau Frète. I picked some grass seeds and chewed on them but they did not help very much. Later I found some wild beans, but they were very hard and I had no fire to cook them, so I put them in my knapsack in case I should find fire somewhere. I thought, "Here I am in the wilderness without anything to eat. Ogoun, help me or I will die." I took out the piece of iron and held it in my open hand. I said aloud, "Ogoun, I am your child. Save me." Then I sang an Ogoun song and marked an Ogoun sign on the earth. After that I sang another song reproaching Ogoun for neglecting me in my difficulties:

> Ogoun Papa, I am your child, why do you forget me?
> Ogoun Papa, I am your horse, why do you neglect me?
> Ogoun in Guinée, Ogoun Beneath the Water, Ogoun of
>   the Nagos,
> Papa Ogoun, I serve you but you forget me.

VII

I sat down on a rock thinking that the wilderness was going to consume me and that it might as well be here as somewhere else. At that very moment I saw an old man coming down the mountainside. Now and then he called out, in the manner of the mountain people, "Whooo-oo!" meaning to attract my attention, and when he arrived he greeted me as if I were a brother or son whom he hadn't seen for a long while. He asked me if I came from the capital city, and I told him no, I had never been to the city, that I lived on another mountain. He said that some of his family had gone to the city and never returned and he wanted to know about them. He asked where I was going and I told him I didn't know any more, and I was too hungry to go any further. He took a small cloth packet from his knapsack and opened it. Inside were a few kernels of roasted maize. He gave me two kernels and I chewed on them. He put one kernel in his mouth, re-wrapped the packet and put it back on his knapsack. Although I was grateful for the two kernels, I was sure they could do nothing to keep me alive. But strangely, after I had chewed and swallowed them my hunger disappeared and I felt much stronger.

He asked me why I was not using the trail, and I told him I did not see any trail. He said, "Over there, just a little way. I was walking up toward my house, when I felt something pushing against my chest. I stopped. I did not see anyone. I asked, 'Who is it?' I heard a voice say, 'It is I, Papa Ogoun. There is a lost boy down below. He belongs to me. Go and find him.' I turned and saw you in the distance, so I came. Do you really serve Ogoun?" I said yes and showed him the piece of iron I had in my knapsack. He told me to come with him and he led me to the trail, and from there we climbed to his house up above.

It was a small house like the one my family lived in, with a tonnelle, a canopy of banana leaves extending outward from the door. Beneath the canopy a woman was cooking something in an iron pot, and two young girls were pounding with long poles in a large wooden mortar. The girls looked at me, then turned away and giggled. The woman said to the old man, "Who is the boy?" He said, "I was on the trail. My vodoun told me there was a lost boy down below and I went down to look for him. There he was, sitting on a rock getting ready to die." The woman looked at me closely, all the while stirring her iron pot. At last she said, "Yes, he looks thin." She went into the house and brought out a piece of cooked plantain for me.

The old man said, "I am going to weed my garden now. Take the hoe and the sickle and follow me." I went with him to the garden and we worked. He said, "You do not know how to hoe. Make the hoe hit like you were drumming for a dance." I thought of a song and made the hoe go as if I were beating a drum to keep time. He said, "Good, now you are hoeing properly," and he began to sing in time to the hoe sounds. The song he sang was for the loa Azaka, protector of farmers, whom everyone called Cousin because he was an habitant like the rest of us. Azaka dressed like other habitants, in blue pantalons and a long blue shirt, wore a head kerchief and a straw hat, and carried a straw knapsack and a machete. The old man's song was telling Cousin that he was weeding his field with his machete and hoe, just as he was supposed to do. It was a very lighthearted song and ended with the words, "If I take a woman and she leaves me, tomorrow I will find another one."

I asked him if the woman at the house was his wife, and he said no, she was his daughter and the two girls were his grand-children. I said, "Papa, I do not know your name." He stood erect and looked around at his garden. He said, "Yes, I did not tell you. It is Prosper Saintvil. That is the name by which I am known, but of course it is not my secret name." I asked, "Papa, what is your secret name?" He looked at me severely and said, "Why do you want to know that?" I said I was just interested to know. He said, "Why should I tell you or anyone else? How do I know you are not a baka?" I said I was not a baka and did not mean to be impolite. He said, "Maybe you are a bakulu." I de-nied that I was a bakulu. He said, "Maybe you are a zeau-beaup." I denied it. He said, "Or a lougaro." I said no, I was just a person. I was traveling here and there in search of my brother. I reminded him that Ogoun had sent him to find me, and that I was one of Ogoun's children.

After thinking about it for a moment, Prosper Saintvil nod-ded his head and resumed working with his machete. He asked me if I had a secret name, and I realized that I had one but rarely thought about it. I said, "Yes, it is . . ." but he stopped me with a stern gesture and said, "Never tell it! There may be bakas hid-ing behind the rocks and trees, and if they hear it you will be in great trouble." I said I never realized it. He went on working without talking, and after a while he stood up and said, "There was an habitant down below. He is not there any more. Some zeaubeaups learned his secret name and he fell into their power. He was on the trail late one night and was passing a mapou tree. He saw light coming from the cracks in the tree. Then the zeaubeaups came out. They surrounded him and danced, singing "You are ours, you are ours!" He waved his cocomacaque at them, but they only laughed. They said, "It is no use, we have your secret name."

I asked Prosper Saintvil what happened to the man. He looked very solemn. He said, "What do the zeaubeaups want with anyone? They wanted to eat him. They said to him, 'We give you your choice. We will eat you as you are, or we will quarter you first and then eat you.' He did not know what to answer, so they took off his clothes and dragged him inside the mapou tree. After that he was never seen again." I never knew it was like that with zeaubeaups and it made me fearful. Prosper Saintvil pondered. He said, "How do we know exactly what happened if the man never was seen again? An old woman was on the same trail that night. She saw it all. In fact she brought back some of the clothes the zeaubeaups had taken from him. There is even more to the story. Two days later was market day in the village. A strange woman was there selling meat. She said she came from a certain place, but no one had ever seen her before. The market women looked at the meat. It did not look like pork or beef, and one woman said she saw a piece of human fingernail on the meat tray. All the women packed up their produce and left the market. The strange woman was the last to go. No one ever saw her again."

I asked Prosper Saintvil, "Is there no protection from zeaubeaups? If a person calls on Legba to protect him, will he do it?" Prosper shook his head. "Perhaps, perhaps not. Legba is powerful but he is unreliable. Perhaps he listens to you, perhaps he doesn't. Even if he hears you he may be indolent about it. That is his character. He doesn't always like to do what he is expected to do, and he often likes to do just the opposite. You have to deal with Legba, but he doesn't have to deal with you. When he appears at a service he may make a man do things that are improper. He may cause him to expose his penis and offer it to women, offending everyone. Invoke Legba, yes, but don't depend on him." I asked, "Is there no other defense against zeaubeaups?" The old man said, "Yes, there are certain ways but I do not know all of them. My uncle told me that one time he was on the road and came to a mapou tree. He heard voices inside and knew they were zeaubeaups. He climbed into the branches of the tree and waited. When the zeaubeaups came out he urinated on them from above and they ran away screaming. My uncle was a Nago man, and he learned about zeaubeaups back in his own country."

We finished our work, we started back to the house, but not before the old man sang his song to Cousin again and sprinkled crumbs from his cornbread on the ground. I asked him about sprinkling the breadcrumbs and he said, "That shows Cousin that I share with him. He works in my garden with me. He makes the crops grow well. He watches over everything. Therefore I share what I have." I asked him about the song he had sung to Cousin, saying I didn't understand the words about losing a woman and finding another one. He laughed and began to sing the song again. This time he danced, just as if he were hearing drums, turning this way and that and making motions with his arms as if he were hoeing, cutting with a sickle, or chopping with a machete. It was a very good dance, and he had a happy smile on his face all the while he was doing it. When he came to the words, "If I take a woman and she leaves me, tomorrow I will find another," he seemed very happy.

I asked again about those words, and he said it was Cousin who was speaking them, not Prosper Saintvil. He said Cousin could be stern and demanding, but usually he was gay and happy and wanted his habitant children to be the same. The meaning of the words was that life goes on, and whatever happens to a person he must not lie down and die but continue to live as the god in the sky meant him to live. I said, "I do not know much about the god in the sky." Prosper said, "No, he is too far away, therefore we do not hold services for him. We just acknowledge him by calling his name." I said a white houngan had told me it was Jesus. He said, "Do not listen. The god in the sky is Mawu, though some call him Lissa or Nananbouclou. They are the same. Also, if you are a Nago person you may call him Olorun. Mawu created the world, and he will take it back whenever he pleases. But we cannot deal with him directly, therefore we speak to our vodouns who are down here where we can talk to them. As for the Frenchman you thought was a houngan or a bocor, he knows nothing but what is written for him in a little book."

Prosper's daughter's name was Élizia. She said I could stay with them for a while and help her father in the field. I was glad of that because I would get something to eat every day. Every morning she gave Prosper and me a cup of coffee and we would go out to work in the garden. When there was no garden work to be done she gave me other tasks to do, like collecting grass and repairing the roof of the house. Sometimes there was nothing to do and I sat around and talked with her daughters. The older one's name was Innomine, and the younger was Morgina. Once in a while Innomine gave me sidelong glances, and once she asked me to go with her to the spring for water. We filled her water jar, but before going home she led me to a hidden place among the rocks and asked me if I wanted to copulate with her. This I did but I felt very uneasy about it, thinking that her mother and Prosper would not like it. Nevertheless we did it on several occasions.

One night Mama Élizia asked me about my brother and his friend, and I told her everything. She asked if some houngan had told me where to look for them. I said no but everyone seemed to think they were somewhere in the mountains. She said, "You appear to be a man but you are only an innocent child. You are wandering around without any idea of where you are going." I said I knew they were alive because a certain houngan had learned it from an ancestor below the water. She said, "Well, you also are alive, but could your brother find you?" What she said discouraged me, but one evening she said, "In a few days we are going to have a service for many vodouns. Perhaps we can get one of them to reveal where your brother and his friend are." I said I would be grateful for that, and I asked her which vodouns would be served. She answered, "Woy! There are many. The one who protects our house is Shango. The one who protects our garden is Cousin. The one served by my father is Ogoun. I myself have two vodouns, Agwé and Imamou. Also, other vodouns will come with them, though I don't know which ones." I thought that one of those vodouns would surely know where my brother was.

After that Mama Élizia kept me with her, and Prosper had to work in the garden by himself. He did not like that, because he enjoyed talking to someone while he was working. One of the things I had to do for Mama Élizia was to go searching for honey, which she needed for the service. I also had to repair the thatching that covered her courtyard, her peristyle, where the dancing would take place. In preparation for her big service to the vodouns, Mama Élizia set up a table inside the house and placed on it all the important ritual things. There was a large

Prosper to work in his garden. I remembered the battle that had taken place over possession of my head and was worried that sometime it might happen again. I asked Prosper about it and he stopped working and leaned on his hoe. He said, "Perhaps it will never happen again. Ogoun drove Gèdé away, so Gèdé will find someone else." I said, "I had a terrible dream after I fell asleep. I dreamed that I was burrowing under the ground like some kind of animal. I burrowed into a grave with a person's bones in it. I kept burrowing but went into another grave with more bones. I burrowed from one grave to another." Prosper looked serious. He said, "That was because of Gèdé. He left the dream in your head to torment you when Ogoun drove him out. But now you have used the dream up. Do not think about it any more."

I began to feel better. After we returned to the house and Mama Élizia fed us she said to me, "Last night when Agwé entered my head he told me things I wanted to know. He spoke of your brother Jean-Jacques and his friend André. He said they are at a plantation called Habitation Perdue." I asked if they were well and she replied, "Agwé told me they are in great difficulty. They are in the power of a man named Gros Ventre. They work on his plantation, which is very large. Gros Ventre's vodoun is Gèdé Mivèvou, the brother of Gèdé Raché who came to you last night. Perhaps Mivèvou sent Raché, who can tell?" I asked where Habitation Perdue was to be found and she said, "Agwé was not clear about it, but it is somewhere in the western mountains beyond Anse-à-Veau." Anse-à-Veau was far away and I became very discouraged.

Prosper Saintvil seemed unhappy that I was leaving, but he gave me advice about the route I should take. He said that I should go down from the mountains to Petit Goâve at the edge of the sea and follow the road to Anse-à-Veau. "Before you quite get to Anse-à-Veau you will come to a river which flows from the mountains. Follow the river upward to its source and I think you will be where you are supposed to go." I was sorry to be going because everyone had been so good to me, just as if I belonged to the family, and I had become very attached to Innomine.

The evening before I left, Prosper took me from the house to a place of dense brush and made me take off my clothes. He rubbed me all over with a lotion he had made, and after I dressed he gave me a medicine packet to hang around my neck. He said, "My daughter has much knowledge, but I am the one who understands how to deal with bakas and lougaros. Throw away your cocomacaque stick, because it has already been defeated by the Red Pigs and now it is dead. Here is a Guinée stick made of chardette wood. It is more powerful. If you strike a baka with it he will fall down crying, and after that he will leave you alone." The Guinée stick had a head carved at the knob end. Prosper said, "The head you see is that of Brisé, who lives in the chardette tree. With one blow he can knock down a great pine. There is a certain mountain in Guinée without any top. People say there was a village of bakas there, and Brisé decided to get rid of it so he knocked off the top of the mountain." I put a cord around my waist and hung the Guinée stick to it. Prosper took my cocomacaque stick and flung it into the bush. He said, "If you ever have to use the Guinée stick, say, "General Brisé, I call you, General Brisé!'"

VIII

In the morning Mama Élizia gave me
some cornbread to put in my knapsack and
I went down the trail, branching off when I
found another trail that would take me toward the sea. As I descended I began to see
more habitations, each with a small white
house, and sometimes I passed women carrying headloads of maize or yams. At one
place my trail crossed another at the foot of
a large tree. When I saw a ring of stones
around the foot of the tree I became wary
and stopped. Then I saw a doll-like figure
made of sticks and cloth, wrapped with rib-
bons, hanging from one of the tree
branches, and also some small objects attached to sticks which were implanted in
the ground near the tree. One of the objects
was a dried toad, another a bundle of black
bird feathers. These objects were called gbo
or ouangas, and they were very dangerous.
I decided not to cross the other trail at that
point and made a wide detour, but I was
not able to find a new trail and went down
the mountain in an arroyo. I found a dry
stream bed below and followed it for a long
distance until I came to a road that was
probably a ford when the water was flowing.

Though I never stopped to rest, whenever I came to a high point the sea seemed as far away as ever. The road brought me to a small compound of houses toward nightfall, and I asked the habitants if I could sleep on the ground in the courtyard. They were not very hospitable at first and asked me many questions, but finally they said I could sleep on the ground. I found some grass to put under me and lay down, but I could not sleep very well because of the cold. I could hear the people talking in their houses and saw the light of their oil lamps coming through cracks in the walls. I said to myself, "Ogoun, these are not good people. They are warm inside and I am cold. They did not even offer me a gourd of water."

I was beginning to feel very sorry about everything when a woman came out of her house and gave me a small piece of melon to eat. She went behind her house and returned with an armful of straw for me to cover myself with. After a while she asked why I was traveling on the road so late in the day and where I was going. I said I was going to Petit Goâve or Mirogoane and had lost my way. She said, "Ah, this road will not take you there. It appears to descend, but it turns and mounts again." I told her I had taken this road only because I wanted to avoid the cross-trail where all the ouangas had been set out under the tree. She nodded, saying "I know the place. I have never been there but people speak of it. A bocor lives in a cave nearby and the ouangas are his. He is constantly making magic against people and sending out expeditions. It is said his house is full of jars that contain the spirits of dead persons that he sends out to do his work against anyone he doesn't like." I asked the name of the bocor, and she said no one knew his true name but he was generally called the Malefactor of Trou Noir. She said I was fortunate to have come along the trail in the daylight and turned away, else something bad surely would have happened to me. When I finished eating the melon, she brought me a gourd of black beans, and after that I was able to sleep a little. In the morning the woman gave me instructions about how I could find the trail to the sea. The other people in the compound were still suspicious and hardly spoke to me, and they seemed glad when I left.

I walked two more days before I reached the sea, but I saw

no town, only a road and, between the road and the water, a small fishing village. I found out that I had already passed Petit Goâve and that Anse-à-Veau was to the west. I was very hungry. I approached an old man and his son who were unloading fish from their boat, and asked them if I could do something to earn a mouthful of food. The old man asked me where I came from, and when I said Morne Rouge his face broke into a wide smile. He said, "Woy, here is a mountain man." Other fishermen and their women gathered round and listened to our conversation. Soon they were all asking questions, and no matter what I said they smiled or laughed. I said to the old man, "Papa, why are they laughing? My stomach is crying out and everyone laughs." He said, "It is because of the way you talk. It is very sing-song. We don't speak the same way down here."

I became angry. I said, "If you came to Morne Rouge would the people laugh at you? No, they would say, 'Here is a gourd of water. Here are some Congo beans to eat.'" I left them and started walking again but paused when I heard someone calling for me to stop. It was a young woman with a basket of plantains on her head. She said, "My house is just over there. I can give you something to eat." I followed her and she told me to sit on the bench by the door. In a few moments she came out of the house with a gourd of akasan for me. When I had eaten it I said, "Mademoiselle, I have only a few copper coins to pay you." She said, "No, not yet. Sit a while. Later you can do a little work for me." I did not make any conversation, for she was satisfied to do all the talking. She told me she had come from Jacmel and found a husband in Petit Goâve. He was a fisherman, and one day there was a storm and his boat did not come back, so now she lived alone. When I was a little refreshed I performed some small tasks for her, like repairing a housepost that had been eaten by beetles. No matter what I was doing she continued to tell me about her life or about other women in the village.

Darkness came and I began to wonder where I was going to sleep. She lighted an oil lamp inside the house and called out, "Come in, here is your sleeping mat." I saw only one sleeping mat and said, "Mademoiselle, that is your mat." She said, "It is mine, it is yours." I accepted it. Later she put out the oil lamp and shared the mat with me. I could not sleep, but discovered that she did not want me to. For a while I forgot altogether about my brother Jean-Jacques and his friend André. Then I slept, and when I awoke cocks were already crowing and dogs were barking, and I could hear the men on the beach with their boats.

I went down to the shore to bathe, and afterwards she gave me coffee with sugar. I did not find out her name until then. It was Félicie Moreau. I told her about where I was going and she looked very serious. She said, "It is a dangerous place, those mountains behind Anse-à-Veau. No one goes there." I said I had to go because my brother was in difficulty and I had to find him. She said there were numerous caves and mapou trees where bakas and lougaros lived. She told me that once when she was on the Anse-à-Veau road she had seen a large party of bakas dancing along the way with drums. It seemed at first as if they were all dressed in white, but as they came closer she saw that they were really formed out of mist and a person could see right through them. She tried to run, but they overtook her and suddenly she was surrounded by the mist bakas. She escaped only because she had a small packet of salt with her. She scattered salt in all directions and the mist bakas faded away and disappeared.

I asked if she had heard of Habitation Perdue and she stopped talking about her encounters with bakas. She said, "Is that what you are looking for? Do not do it." I told her it was revealed to me by a mambo that my brother was at that place. She said, "Poor devil. Then he is a zombie." I said no, the mambo only told me that he was in trouble. She replied, "What greater trouble is there in the world? If he is a zombie you cannot help him." I brooded for a while, and she said she was going to bring someone who knew about Habitation Perdue.

She went out, and when she returned, the old fisherman I had met on the beach when I first arrived was with her. She said his name was Dumé La France. She set out coffee for him and he sat down and looked at me very seriously. He said, "Is it true that you are on your way to Habitation Perdue?" I said I believed my brother was there and I was looking for him. He shook his head and said, "No one goes there willingly. Those who do never return. Go back where you came from." I asked what was so terrible about Habitation Perdue. He said, "I have never seen it. If I had, I would not be here. But I have heard many things. Gros Ventre lives there. My father told me about him when I was only a boy. He is an evil creature. Some people call him Great Devil Bocor, some say Devil Demon. He is a baka.

"A cousin of my father discovered Habitation Perdue by accident. Most of the people were zombies, some working in the field, some doing nothing. They took hold of my father's cousin and brought him to Gros Ventre. There was a large wooden mortar in front of his house and two women zombies were pounding in it with large pestles. Gros Ventre said, 'Ah, you are just in time. I need more heads for the mortar.' My father's cousin looked into the mortar and saw that the women were pestling human heads. He became very fearful. He got down on his knees, he groveled on the ground, begging Gros Ventre not to do that to him. Gros Ventre said, 'I did not invite you to come here, you chose to come. Anyone who comes to Habitation Perdue has to stay.'

"My father's cousin asked why it was necessary to stay and Gros Ventre said, 'Why, if I let someone leave he would go here and there telling everything he has seen here, and that would cause me a great deal of trouble. People would come looking for relatives and friends.' My father's cousin protested, 'No, no, I would say nothing! "The eyes see, the mouth is sealed." It is a solemn promise! If I lie, let Hevioso strike me with his thunderbolt! If I lie, let Gèdé on the Graveyard take me! If I lie, let the Vodoun of Smallpox have me and my body will be thrown in a ravine! If I lie, let Agwé of the sea take me below water! If I lie, let Tijean Pétro who hides in the coconut palm eat me!' Gros Ventre answered, 'Your oath is a strong one. Very well, I will let you go if you perform a service for me. You will take one of my zombies to the habitation of my brother, Maigre Ventre, who lives in the next valley.' And my father's cousin said, 'Yes, yes, I will do it.'

"Gros Ventre sent for the zombie and a man brought him tied to a long banana-leaf rope. My father's cousin took the end of the rope and walked the zombie across the mountain until they arrived at the habitation of Gros Ventre's brother. After that my father's cousin ran away as fast as he could and never returned to that part of the country. The only one he told about the affair was my father, and my father told me. That is how I came to know about it."

It was hard for me to stop thinking about the zombie women pounding human heads in the mortar, but I said to Dumé La France, "If all these things happened in the days of your father and his cousin, why, it must have been before the time of Dessalines." He said, "Yes, perhaps it was so." I said, "Then surely Gros Ventre long ago grew old and died, and Habitation Perdue is no longer there." He shook his head, "Ah, my child, you do not understand. Gros Ventre is not just a man. He is not just an ordinary bocor. He is a baka, a lougaro, a devil. He appears to be human but he is not. People like us live and die, but Gros Ventre lives on and on and never grows older. Habitation Perdue is not simply another plantation but a terrible place where all the labor in the fields is done by zombies. Zombies do not survive forever, and whenever Gros Ventre's zombies are used up he sends out expeditions to gather more. Before Dessalines, before Toussaint he was there. Some of his zombies are French, some Spanish, some English, some Taino. There are black men like you, mulattoes, even albinos. If you go there you will never come back." I said, "If I do not go there, how will I find my brother?" Dumé said, "If that is truly where he is, your brother is lost and you cannot do anything to help him."

Dumé was silent for a while. I could see that he was thinking of something else. At last he said, "Also, there are the bizangos. Between here and where you are going they say there are many of them." I had heard of bizangos but knew very little about them. I said, "Papa, I don't know about bizangos. My father never mentioned them." Dumé seemed surprised. "You are a mountain man and you don't know about them? They can be anywhere in the mountains. You are walking on a trail in the evening. The sun is going down, the daylight begins to grow dim, but it is not yet dark, just beginning. You feel that something is there but you do not see anything. You look behind you, nothing. You look toward the sea, nothing. You look toward the hills, nothing. Then ahead of you are glistening spots of light. They are the eyes of bizangos coming toward you. They approach. You see that they resemble huge dogs. There is a large pack of them, maybe ten or twelve. They sit down across the trail, their tongues hanging from their mouths and dripping saliva. You throw a stone but they do not run. They spread out and surround you. They are hungry and you are their food."

Dumé waved his machete and said, "They are not dogs but bizangos. What are bizangos? They are a secret society of a certain kind of bakas. During the day they resemble ordinary people. They farm their gardens and journey to the market. But all the same, they are demons. They have meetings in caves to talk about whether they will do this or that. They can take on forms of different animals. But when it is time to go hunting they transform themselves into huge wild dogs. If you had a gun it wouldn't help you. Bullets pass through them as if they were made of air, and they do not bleed. Only people protected by the Congo vodoun Moundongue are safe. Others disappear and are never heard of again. No ordinary houngan or bocor can give you protection. Only a Moundongue priest can help you. He makes a service and gives you a piece of dog's tail to hang from your neck. If you do not have that you are lost." He went back to his boat to work and did not say anything more.

IX

For several days after that I did not do anything except walk along the shore or do little jobs for Félicie. I even pestled grain for her and carried water as if I were a child or a woman. But my mind was on my journey and the dangers I might encounter on the way to Habitation Perdue. It seemed to me that I was too small and insignificant for such a task. It was a job for a powerful bocor, not a young man like me. I thought, "If I meet bizangos what will I do? If I meet bakas what will I do? If I ever get to Gros Ventre's place what will I do then? If my brother and André have been transformed into zombies, what can I do to save them? One way or another I will surely die. If bizangos do not get me, zeaubeaups will." I thought I ought to return home and help my father farm his fields.

Félicie kept urging me to stay with her and be a fisherman, but finally she saw it was no use, and when we were eating our boiled cornmeal and fish one evening she said, "I know a Moundongue woman." I wondered how that could be of any importance. Félicie said, "I think she understands about bizangos." We went together to the old woman's house on the road to Petit

Goâve. The woman's name, Félicie told me, was Mama Musoka, and she was very strange but people believed she had special powers. When we arrived, Mama Musoka was eating rice from a small gourd. She did not greet us but went on eating. Her eyes gleamed in the lamplight and kept moving back and forth from Félicie's face to mine.

At last she said in a thick cracked voice, "This is a Moundongue house. What do you Nagos want here?" Félicie said very respectfully, "Mama, we are not Nagos. This boy has to go up the mountain to find his brother but he is worried about bizangos." The old woman answered angrily, "Ah, bizangos. When people want something from me I see them, otherwise I do not see them. Do I have sons to fish and collect crabs for me? No. Does anyone ever bring me a red snapper or a conch? No. They say, 'Let that old woman go foraging and find wild rice.' They say, 'She is so small and withered she cannot be very hungry anyway.' But if they need something they come saying, 'Mama Musoka, Mama Musoka.'" Félicie said, "Mama Musoka, I don't have a man or children to help me either. It is a hard life." Mama Musoka became more agitated. She said, "Oh, you poor young one. You do not know what hard means. Wait until you are as old as I am, then you will know. Better than that, throw yourself in the ocean and do not grow old."

Félicie said, "Mama, I will see that you get some red snappers and conches to eat. I promise it. Just tell this boy what he can do to cope with bizangos when he is in the mountains." Mama Musoka said, "Why should I know anything about bizangos?" Félicie said, "Why, only because bizangos come from Moundongue country in Guinée." The old woman narrowed her eyes and said, "Are you going to blame bizangos on my people?" Félicie said, "Mama, I do not know anything about such things. But many people say that Moundongues have special power over bizangos." Mama Musoka held the oil lamp higher to see my face. She said, "He is very young. Let him go home." I said, "Mama, I think sometimes I should, but I cannot sleep for thinking of my brother."

At last Mama Musoka raised herself up and walked lamely to a dark part of the room. When she returned she was holding a short piece of a dried dog's tail. She put it on the table and sang something in the Moundongue language. I heard her sing "Moundongue oh, yè yè yè," but I didn't understand anything else. When she was finished she gave me the piece of dog's tail and told me to fasten it inside my shirt. She said, "Maybe it will protect you, maybe not. After all, am I a Nago? Am I a Daho-mean? Am I a mambo or a bocor? Who am I to know anything worthwhile? I am only a hungry old woman who has been thrown away."

We thanked her for the gift, and I promised to bring her something to eat the next day. The following morning I walked along the shore to gather shellfish and I traded some clams for a red snapper. I put everything in a basket and brought it to Mama Musoka's house. She spoke crossly to me, but her eyes told me she was glad. She made me sit down at the table and she brought out an object wrapped in cloth. She unwrapped it and I saw it was a Congo packet covered with beads. She put it in the center of the table and talked to it in Moundongue lan-guage. A moment later a different voice came from her mouth as if from a great distance. Then her voice again, then the other voice. She picked up the packet and rewrapped it. She said, "I have spoken to them, the bizangos, and told them to leave you alone or Nzambi would be angry. Nzambi is the great sky spirit of our people. They listened. They said they would try to re-member. If they do not, show them the dried dog's tail."

I said, "Mama Musoka, I am grateful to you. But I did not know you were a mambo." She said, "I am neither one thing nor another, but I belong to the Moundongue nation. I do not know everything, but whatever is Moundongue I know, even if I am only a hungry old woman. Tell Félicie to bring me another red snapper soon." I told her I would tell Félicie, and I went back to the fishing village.

The next morning when I woke up I was not thinking any more about going home and I was ready to go on searching for my brother. I laid out all my magical protections on the sleeping mat. There were the things Kuku Cabrit had given me—the fragment of Ogoun's iron, the medicine packet I wore on my chest, the colored beads, and the divining cord to use in case I became lost. The cocomacaque baton he had given me was gone, because it had been neutralized by the Red Pigs and I had thrown it away, but I now had the Guinée stick made of chardette wood for me by Prosper Saintvil. I also had the dried dog's tail from Mama Musoka. The passport Bocor Zandolite had given me with the vodoun signs written on it had been burned by the white man in robes who gave me the words "Father, Son and Holy Spirit." I still had his small cross, though I didn't think it was very worthwhile. Nevertheless I kept it, since it resembled Legba's crossroad sign. I put everything in its proper place, either around my neck or under my shirt or in my knapsack, except for the Guinée stick which I hung from my waist cord, and Félicie saw that I was ready to leave.

She said, "Well, you are going after all. I thought you would stay and we could make our living together. Perhaps when you get halfway to Habitation Perdue you will change your mind and come back. Maybe I will be here, maybe not. Maybe I'll have another man by then. But if you go all the way and too many things happen to you, if you are half eaten or your limbs are withered, that's not the kind of man for me." I said I didn't have any idea of what would happen but I expected that in time she would see me again coming from the direction of Anse-à-Veau. When I left she was winnowing grain.

I saw Dumé La France working on his boat and I went to say good-bye to him. He was carving a dowel and he barely looked at me. I said, "Papa, I am going now." He answered, "So you are really going to that place? It is a wild journey. Do not let the vodoun in your head fall asleep." I said, "My vodoun is Ogoun. They say he never sleeps." He picked up a shell and threw it into the water. "All vodouns sleep, sometimes when you want them most. You have to keep them awake." I answered, "Yes, Papa." He said, "The road to Anse-à-Veau is a bad one. Sometimes it is only a stony trail. Sometimes the ocean comes up and washes it away altogether. The best thing is to go as far as you can by boat."

I told Dumé I didn't have a boat and had no money to pay for a ride. He looked along the shore toward where a family was gathered around a small fishing boat. He said, "That is Aubelin

Saline over there. He is going to Ville Cochon for a wedding. Maybe he will take you that far." He called out, "Aubelin! You see this young man here? He is my nephew from the Red Mountains. His name is Dosu. He is going to Anse-à-Veau. I told him you would take him as far as Ville Cochon." Aubelin answered, "No, I have my whole family, I can't take anyone else." Dumé said, "Didn't you hear me say he is my nephew? That makes him part of your family." Aubelin said, 'How can he be part of my family? I never saw him before."

Dumé said gravely, "Think what you are saying. You are married to my cousin Voluska's oldest daughter. Therefore you are related to this boy Dosu." Aubelin answered, "I never heard that you had a nephew named Dosu." Dumé said, "Do I tell you everything I know? I tell you only a little, because your head couldn't contain any more and everything would spill out. Listen. I have a half-brother up in the mountains. He is a big houngan. This is his oldest son. You are going to a wedding and should have a generous spirit. Take him with you as far as Ville Cochon." Aubelin said, "How much will he pay?" Dumé said, "Pay? You want the son of my brother to pay something?" Aubelin said, "Very well, I will take him but he will have to feed himself."

Dumé gave me three pieces of sugar cane to chew on if I got hungry. I thanked him for his help and he said, "Never mind about that. I just want to see Aubelin do something useful sometimes." As I left, he said, "Remember what I told you about bizangos." I climbed into the boat with Aubelin. It was very crowded, with seven people in all. Aubelin's two sons pushed the boat from the shore with their oars, then climbed in and rowed until the sail caught a small breeze. Aubelin held the tiller. We headed straight to sea until the sail filled out, then veered west. Aubelin's two small granddaughters kept asking me if there was an ocean like this up in the mountains where I came from. When I said no, we didn't have any ocean up there they seemed pleased.

Aubelin was silent at first, but when he saw I didn't know anything about sailing a boat he began to talk. He said, "You see that blue banner at the top of the mast? That is for Imamou, for all the Imamou family." I acknowledged that I didn't know anything about Imamou. He said, "Wye! You are really from the mountains. Imamou is the spirit of the ocean. He guides us wherever we are going. He takes us where the fish are and puts them in our nets. When we say Imamou we really mean all his family. There is Agwé, he is the fiercest one. He causes thunder and storms. Also there are Agwètta, Agwèsu Wandéou, La Sirène, and others."

I said we had different vodouns up in the mountains, and he said, "Yes, mountain people don't know too much. Probably you never heard of Yzolé either." I said, "Yes, I have heard of it." He said, "Yzolé is down below the ocean. At a certain place out there, a good day's sailing, two great rivers come together under the water. That is where Yzolé is. It is a big town, bigger than Jacmel or Port-au-Prince. Imamou and his whole family live in Yzolé. Other mystères live there as well, but the Imamou nation is the most important." I said, "Thank you, Papa, for telling me. But up in the mountains we call that place Zilé." He said, "Oh, that is what you call it? Some people call it that but it is not the right name. If you want to know something, that place has many names, such as Limonziles and Embouchire and Dleau Contré. But the real name is Yzolé, and if you don't call it properly, Imamou gets angry." I said, "Thank you, Papa, for telling me." I felt very ignorant and wondered how I would ever find my brother and his friend. The world was too complicated.

When the sun was halfway up in the sky the wind stopped blowing and our sail became slack. Aubelin's sons rowed straight out to sea. They had to row a long time before we found a breeze, and then the sails went slack again. The family sat patiently but nothing changed. Aubelin said, "Imamou is sleeping. Let us ask for help from the sky nation." One of his sons brought out a small drum and began beating it. Aubelin's wife sang a song asking for the vodoun Loko to help. The entire family joined. They sang, "Wind, wind, wind, Loko, Aubelin asks for wind." After a while there was a slight breeze and Aubelin guided the boat further from shore. Then a good wind sprang up and we again headed west.

We arrived at Ville Cochon late in the day. Aubelin's relatives met us at the shore and helped draw the boat part way onto the beach. Ville Cochon was not really a village but a small fishing settlement. I asked where I could find the road to Anse-à-Veau, and after thanking Aubelin and his family I left them. I was hungry and began chewing on my sugar cane. Walking was difficult because the road had been washed out by the sea. Several times I saw women riding donkeys loaded with charcoal. As it became darker I saw no one at all and looked for a place to lie down for the night. I walked quite a way in moonlight before I saw a small house on a knoll. It turned out to be deserted, and I lay on the floor without a mat. The mosquitoes were very bad, but I did not have any embers to make a fire to drive them away, and I didn't sleep very much. In the morning I left as soon as the sun came up.

I found a mango tree growing at the edge of the road and threw stones trying to knock down some fruit, but then I heard a voice calling from somewhere above, "Who is stealing mangoes from my tree?" I could not see anyone and became fearful, thinking the tree belonged to a baka. So I stopped throwing stones, but I found one mango that had already fallen and I took it and hurried away. I walked a long distance without seeing anyone or any houses or gardens. The road was so flooded in some places that I took a side trail to higher ground. It seemed to be going west toward the river I was looking for, so I continued with it even though it veered away from the sea. After a while I was no longer able to hear the surf.

I met a young girl on the trail and asked her where she was coming from. She said there was a compound higher up named Terre Glissé, Slippery Earth. I had never heard of a place by that name, and began to worry because in our own mountains whenever people said slippery earth they meant a place where accidents were likely to happen. But there was no other trail, and I wanted to get to some kind of habitation before dark so I went ahead. I saw a small garden here and there, and suddenly as I went over a rise I saw a group of houses in a small dale. Women and girls were pestling grain, but the men weren't doing any kind of work. Instead, they were sitting on benches or on the ground playing a game on wooden boards.

When they saw me approaching, they greeted me enthusiastically. One white-bearded man urged me to sit on his bench and play his game with him. I told him I was very tired, and that I didn't know how to play his game. He said it was called Caille or Wari and was very simple. I asked him if I might have something to drink first, and he sent a small girl into the house for a gourd of water for me. After I drank he said, "Now let us play." The gameboard had pockets carved in it, and every hole had some beans. He began moving beans around from one hole to another and every once in a while he said, "There, I eat you." Men from the other benches came to watch, and they were standing all around us. I was told to move the beans in a certain manner, but then the white-bearded man would stop me, saying, "Too bad, too bad, you did not eat anything." He would pick up beans and play, frequently calling out, "I eat you, I eat you," and everyone would laugh.

He was taking many beans from the board and putting them in a pile in front of him. I said, "Papa, excuse me, but I have been walking all day and I am tired and hungry. I do not have the strength to play." He became angry and said some harsh words. But I would not play any more. The other men also appeared to be angry. I noticed for the first time that the white-bearded man had a light-colored line running from his hair down the ridge of his nose all the way to his chin. Then I saw that the other men also had this line running down their faces. I suddenly realized that these people were lougaros, and the lines were where they split open their skin when they went out of their bodies at night to molest or prey on humans. I was very fearful and the only thing I could think about was how to get out of Terre Glissé as soon as possible. I said, "Papa, forgive me, I am weak because of my journey and because I have not had much to eat. If I could rest a little while I would have the strength to play the game. It is a very interesting game and I would like to learn how to play it better." He said, 'Well, I will give you a little while, but do not take too much time because I have other things to do when it gets dark. Over at the edge of that garden are some banana leaves. You can lie down there and rest until I send someone to get you." I said, "Yes, Papa, thank you, Papa." But he did not offer me anything to eat. So I went and lay down on the banana leaves.

I took out my piece of Ogoun's iron and clutched it in my hand, and in a low voice I called Ogoun's name, "Ogoun, Ogoun, Ogoun." There was no sign that he was listening and I became very desperate and discouraged. But a few moments later I heard shouting at Terre Glissé and I could see people racing in and out of their houses. Then I saw smoke from one of the gardens on the mountainside. People were calling, "Fire up above, fire up above!" Everyone was carrying a hoe or a machete and running as fast as possible to put the fire out. While they were going up the mountain the roof of one of the houses started to burn, and some of the people turned and came back. The confusion was great. I jumped up and ran as fast as I could through a stony gully.

I did not care which way I was going, only that I was getting away from that place of lougaros. When it began to get dark I threw myself on the ground in a grove of pines because I could not run any more. I wondered if the lougaros would be coming after me, but I did not hear or see anything. I thought about the fires at Terre Glissé and realized that Ogoun had set them to give me a chance to escape. I said, "Merci Papa Ogoun" over and over again. I am sure he heard me, because the sun gave off a brilliant red glow from the other side of the mountain just before the daylight faded away.

That night I slept near the gully in a patch of citronelle grass. Citronelle was not liked by mosquitoes, and so I was not bitten very much. But before morning came there was a heavy downpour of rain, and since I had no cover over me I became very wet. When at last the sun came up I lay down on some warm rocks to dry out.

X

I could not find any trails and so I decided to go down to the main road again. There were people on the road now, women with headloads or riding on donkeys, and sometimes a man carrying a tree branch or maybe just a machete or hoe. I asked one old man how far it was to Anse-à-Veau, and he said, "Not far, just a little past the river." But he didn't tell me how far the river was. I walked a long while before reaching the river. The road ended there, and people had to ford through the water. Most of the people took off all their clothes, rolled them in a bundle and tied the bundle to a stick. Then they would go through the river, which was quite deep in the middle, holding the sticks in the air over their heads. When they reached the opposite shore they would dry themselves out in the sun and then get dressed again. Somebody told me there was a shallower ford up above, but it was too far to go, and unless a woman was carrying a small baby she preferred to come this way.

According to the directions given to me by Prosper Saintvil I was not supposed to cross the river but to follow it upward towards its source. Up there somewhere I would find Habitation Perdue. My journey was so difficult that I sometimes forgot why I was making it. I was so hungry at this moment that I didn't even think about the Habitation, only about how I could get something to eat. There was an old woman at the ford with a lame donkey. She had taken the saddle baskets off, but she could not get the donkey to put its lame leg on the ground. She scolded the animal, whipped him, even invoked her vodoun, but the donkey would not move. She began to recite her miseries in a loud voice for everyone to hear. I thought I might be able to carry one of the baskets, which were full of charcoal, a certain distance in exchange for something to eat, and I made this proposal to her.

She said, "Carry one basket? Who will carry the other? And who will carry the donkey?" Some other women gathered around us to give advice, and one of them said, "Let the boy take one basket for you. Leave the donkey and one basket here, and send someone in your family back for them." She argued with them as if they were insulting her, but finally agreed to do it that way. She hitched the donkey to a tree and put the smaller basket on the ground beside it. Some of the women lifted the heavier basket to my head. I expected the old woman to begin walking so that I could follow her, but instead she went behind me and prodded me with a stick as if I were her donkey. So we started out, going back the way I had just come. She did not say anything to me, but she talked to the world telling how unfortunate she was. I felt sorry for her but I didn't like the way she prodded me whenever someone passed by, as if she were telling them I was her donkey. Charcoal dust filtered through the basket and I became very black.

We went a long distance and I feared we were going all the way to Petit Goâve, but finally we turned off on a side trail and came to her house. She said, "Put the basket down here," but she did not help me with it and so I spilled some of the charcoal, for which she scolded me sharply. I felt very weak from the exertion and hunger, but she was not in a hurry to give me something to eat. I sat on the bench by her doorway for quite a while. In her own good time she made a fire and cooked some plantains and black beans for me. After I had eaten I thanked her and started back toward the river, but I did not reach the ford until late afternoon. The first thing I did was to wash the charcoal dust from my body. I saw that many people were camping there for the night. So I begged an ember from a woman and made a fire for myself. I fell asleep quickly and did not wake up until nearly sunrise.

When I arose I decided I would have to carry difé with me and give more thought to feeding myself. I found a broken clay water jug, put some embers in it from the ashes of my fire, and covered them with some dry moss. I had three copper coins left, and bought a little shelled corn which I put in my knapsack. Then I started up the river along a muddy trail without looking back. It was not long before the trail disappeared, but I continued on my way, keeping my direction by staying within sight of the river. Two or three times I saw some zagoutis and so I picked up a stone and carried it in my hand in case I should come close enough to kill one. It was almost mid-day before that happened. I was very fortunate and hit the zagouti on my first try. So I stopped where I was, lighted a fire from my difé, cleaned the zagouti, and cooked it. I ate a good meal and put the rest of the meat in my knapsack.

By late afternoon I had climbed quite a distance and could look back and see the ocean below. Whenever I became thirsty I went to the river and drank. I felt better now with meat in my stomach, and my courage began to return. Once more I was able to think about my brother, and was sure that somewhere ahead of me I would find him. By the time night fell I had not encountered a single human being within speaking distance, though I had seen several distant habitations on the mountainside.

I made a fire, ate a little zagouti meat, and slept on a bed of citronelle grass. When I awoke I was startled to see an old man with a beard and long hair standing nearby watching me. Though I jumped up and greeted him, he did not say anything, just turned and walked away. I followed him, hoping he could give me some information about my route, but he suddenly disappeared in a small grove of trees and I was unable to find him. I became a little anxious, thinking that he might be some kind of a baka. All I could find in the grove was a hole under some stones like the entrance to a rabbit burrow, and I wondered if the man might have been one of those creatures who live below the ground as rabbits or rats and take on the form of humans when they come out. It was confusing to me, because there was also a place below the earth called Ville en bas Terreà, a kind of a city where the people lived like humans until they came up through holes in the ground and turned into rabbits or turkeys or some other animals.

But I admonished myself, saying here I was going up the mountain to rescue my brother from Habitation Perdue and I was nervous because of a rabbit burrow I had found. So I got down on my knees and shouted into the burrow, "Pinga! Beware! I am Dosu Bordeaux. I am not afraid of you! Ogoun protects me! I cannot be poisoned! Bullets cannot kill me! Take care! I cannot be pushed around!" And suddenly, even before I was finished with my announcement, a strong wind came swirling out of the burrow and I heard many voices shouting at me from inside. I didn't understand what they were saying, but I ran back to where I had slept in the citronelle grass, gathered up all my things and departed as quickly as I could.

Later that morning I found a trail that seemed to parallel the river and I followed it. In the distance I could sometimes see small houses and gardens on the mountainside. In the afternoon I met a man cutting a tree not far from the trail, and I stopped to ask him if I was going in the right direction for Habitation Perdue. He answered, "Whooo! Why are you going there?" I said I was looking for my brother. He shook his head and went back to his woodcutting without saying another word. Since he would not speak to me, I resumed my way, and it was evening before I saw any other people. There was a small compound of houses near the trail, and a woman was tending a cooking fire in the middle of the courtyard. Two young girls were pestling grain in a large wooden mortar, and a small baby was crawling on the ground among several white chickens. When the girls at the mortar saw me they threw down their pestles and ran away, and the woman at the fire looked up in surprise as if no strangers ever came this way. She said, "Woy!

Who are you?" I said I was Dosu Bordeaux, I was going up the mountain, and could I please have a little gourd of water.

After she gave me the gourd of water she went to a nearby hollow log and struck it several times with a heavy stick. The sounds went out across a gorge and echoed back from a range of hills in the distance. I didn't know what the sounds were saying, but I knew she was calling someone. After a while a man with a hoe appeared. He looked at me intently, then went into one of the houses without saying anything. The two young girls came back, giggled a little, and resumed pestling in the mortar. I remembered the story I had heard about the pestling of human heads at Habitation Perdue and could not resist looking into the mortar. Of course there was nothing but maize in it, and the girls giggled again. The woman scolded them for bad manners. She said to me, "Is this the first time you ever saw the inside of a mortar? What are you looking for?"

I said, "No, Mama, I was just looking." She said, "Well, while you are doing nothing else bring me one of those branches for the fire." There was a small pile of branches near the house and I brought her one. She moved the iron pot from the three stones it sat on and said, "Put the wood in." I asked, "Where shall I put it?" She said, "There, where that one branch is consumed." I slid the branch into the embers until it almost met the ends of the other two branches, then she replaced the pot, saying, "Well, at least you know how a fire is made." I said, "Yes, Mama, where I come from we make fires the same way." She said, "Zeau-Keau-Teau." I said, "Excuse me, Mama?" The girls laughed and the woman said, "That is what we call three-point fire. One branch is called Zeau, one is called Keau, one is called Teau." I said, "I did not know it." The woman said, "They are three men from villages far apart. They meet on the trail. They put their heads close together. They exchange gossip. The closer their heads get, the hotter the fire. That is why we keep pushing the branches toward the center, to keep them talking." Just then the man came out of the house. He said, "That is the way women tell it. Men do not gossip, only women gossip. Men exchange news. The real name of that three point fire is Prété Soleil, Borrowed from the Sun. It was the vodoun Hevioso who showed us to how to make it. With that kind of fire we can melt copper or iron." I said, "I did not know it."

Suddenly the man said, "Where are you going?" By this time I was reluctant to mention the words Habitation Perdue because I had learned that people didn't like to hear it. So I said, "I am going up the river to look for my brother." He asked, "Does he live up there?" I said, "No, he lives in the mountains above Dleau Frète." He shook his head. "I never heard of it." I said, "It is back there in the east." He shook his head again. "Why are you looking in this direction? There is nothing up the river, only small habitations." I decided not to tell everything I knew, and did not mention anything about how I had learned where to look for Jean-Jacques and André LaFitte. I said only that I had heard from some people that Jean-Jacques was in the mountains above the source of the river. He looked at me sharply and said again, "There is nothing there, only a few un-tamed bakas. I can tell you that with certainty. I know because I am a leaf doctor, and I sometimes travel up there to find partic-ular leaves and roots."

I said that of course I could be mistaken, but that several people had told me and I felt obliged to look. The man said, "Well, I think they were mistaken unless he happens to be a hairy baka." I said I didn't know about hairy bakas. He said, "They live only in those mountains above the river. They are in the form of humans, but they have long beards and are covered all over with long hair. They have their own village and gar-dens. Sometimes they capture humans and make them do all the work that has to be done, like clearing the fields, hoeing and cutting wood." After a moment he added, "Perhaps someone told you your brother was taken by the hairy bakas?" I said, "No, Papa, this is the first time I ever heard of them." I could tell from his eyes that he was looking inside me trying to per-ceive the things I had not spoken about, but I did not say any more, and in a little while he turned and went back into the house.

The woman said, "Everyone speaks about the hairy bakas, but I don't know if they are really there." I told her I thought I had seen one earlier that day, though he just looked like a man with a beard and long hair. I told her how he had disappeared, and about the rabbit burrow. She looked concerned and fell silent. She did speak for quite a while, then she said suddenly, "I believe my husband knows why you are going up above. So do I. You are looking for a certain plantation. Do not do it. Turn back and go home. If your brother is there you cannot do anything for him and you will come to harm. Go back to Dleau Frète."

I said, "Mama, you are very wise to know where I am going. Yes, I am going there to that place. I have to go because I was told in a dream that I am the one who must bring my brother and his friend home." She said, "But when you see your brother, if you ever get there, he may not recognize you. Perhaps he will not even remember his own name. He may not understand anything you say. Probably he will not be able to talk our language any more. The overseer who is in charge of those people speaks to them in a secret language, telling them to do this or do that. A few answer, 'Oui, Mon General,' but most do what they are told without saying anything. When darkness comes they are herded to their miserable huts and fed a little something. Then you might think they would sleep. But they do not sleep. They just sit on benches without moving as if they were dead people. There is no spirit inside their bodies. Their souls have been extracted. They do not have vodouns in their heads. They are hollow. Your brother, if you find him you will not want him."

What this woman told me discouraged me. After I thought about it a while I knew I would have to go for Jean-Jacques even if he was merely a hollow body. I said, "Thank you, Mama, for telling me. Still, if I can bring my brother home, perhaps our houngan can transform him back to what he was." She said, "Houngans can't do that sort of thing. It is too much for them. It has nothing to do with serving the vodouns." I said I had heard that if you made a zombie eat some salt his memory would come back. She said, "Yes, some people say that, but I do not believe it is really so." She was silent again and worked at her chores. When she was finished she sat on the bench by the door of the house and looked toward the mounting hills and ridges to the south. She said, "I doubt that you could ever get there. There are too many dangers on the way. There is the evil Pied Coupé, Leg Cut Off. Some people say he is a vodoun. That may be true, because I have heard his name mentioned in a ritual service. Some people think he is not a vodoun but a terrible demon. He does not go around on the ground because he cannot travel well on one leg. He sits in a tree and waits for strangers to come his way. He has many assistants who serve him. If they catch a human being they bring him to Pied Coupé. He orders them to cut off one of the person's legs, and they roast it over an open fire and eat it.

"There are other dangers also, but I cannot tell you every-thing in one day. How do I know these things are true? I know. My husband is a leaf doctor. He goes everywhere, even beyond that farthest ridge, searching for leaves and roots. He has seen these things with his own eyes. Believe what you want, doubt what you want, it is your affair." I said, "Mama, I believe what you say. Thank you for telling me. I did not know the journey would be so dangerous." She said, "Yes, Dosu Bordeaux, go home." I sat for a long time without saying anything. The woman felt sorry for me and gave me a gourd of rice from the pot. Her husband came out of the house and she gave him a gourd of rice also.

The next house in the lacour was not very far away. An old man was sitting in front of it all the time we were talking, watching us and seeming to listen. While I was eating my rice, he got up with the aid of his cane and walked with great diffi-culty to join us. He lowered himself onto the bench and said to the woman, "Élizia, you know something but not everything. The boy is right about the salt. When I was young I was on the trail with a friend of mine, Jeudi Moron, and his father. At a certain place we met a woman. She was not carrying anything and did not seem to be going anywhere. She was just standing in the trail. When we greeted her she did not hear us. Her clothes were tattered and dusty. Her arms just hung down and did not move. Jeudi's father stood right in front of her but she didn't see him. She was a zombie, but how she got there we could not guess.

"Jeudi's father took her arm and stretched it straight out from her shoulder. When he let go, her arm stayed that way as if she were made of wood. He said, 'Madame, where are you going and where are you coming from?' She did not speak. He moved her arm down to her side again and said to us, 'She is a zombie. She hears nothing and sees nothing.' Then he looked in his knapsack and found a small packet of salt. He took some of the salt in his fingers and forced it between her lips. After a few moments she began to tremble. She seemed to see Jeudi's father for the first time. She fell to the ground and began to wail. She called out, 'Oh misère! Oh misère! I am Larose Danzon! Help me, help me!' We did not know what to do. But suddenly she jumped to her feet and began running. She left the trail and went into the brush. Jeudi and I wanted to follow her, but his father said, 'No, let her go. If we catch her, how can we help? We should just spread the word that Larose Danzon is out here. Perhaps her relatives will hear about it and come after her.' That is what happened. Her relatives in the village heard about it and found her and took her home. I was there. I saw it all. That is how I know about the salt."

The woman, whose name I now knew to be Élizia, did not say anything, but I could tell from her eyes that she did not accept what the old man told us. He started talking again about zombies. He said that one sure way to identify a zombie was to watch the mosquitoes. If a mosquito alights on a zombie and pierces his skin, he said, it quickly withdraws its stinger and flies away. If it stays long enough to take some blood it will fall dead. "Therefore," the old man said, "we have the saying, 'Mosquito beware the zombie.'" Élizia said, "Perhaps it is so, but we do not need mosquitoes to tell us when we see a zombie."

The old man said, "I heard everything you were telling the boy about what he may find on the way to that certain place up above. But you forgot to mention the donkey baka and their village, Lacour Bourriques. Do you know about them? If they catch a person they use him as a horse and make him carry them around." I asked if there were bizangos up there, and he said, "Yes, many, and other things too such as the Grey Pigs.

They are worse than the Red Pigs." He went on talking about various kinds of bakas and demons, but I didn't want to hear about them and stopped listening.

They talked then about other things, and I began to wonder where I was going to sleep. When the old man got up to go home he motioned me to come with him. He was the only person living in his house and he gave me a banana-leaf mat to sleep on. But he himself did not lie down right away. He seemed to be glad to have someone to talk to. He said, "I am Hector Soubré. This lacour, it is my family that owns it. Élizia is my oldest daughter. I have a younger daughter who went away to live in the town. The other houses belong to my three sons and their families. When I became too old to work, they took over my gardens. Sometimes I work with my leaf doctor son-in-law to make lotions and medicines. I was never a leaf doctor, exactly, but my father taught me a great deal and I learned from him how to make potions for curing. I gave my son-in-law some old secrets about herb doctoring. You, young man, do you have sores or worms? I can do something for you."

I said, "No, Grandfather, but I thank you. It is other things that trouble me. I wonder if I will ever get to Habitation Perdue." The old man jumped to his feet, exclaiming, "No! Never mention that name! Just say, 'That certain place.' If you say the name aloud it floats out in the air and is heard at that certain place, and the master of the place sends an expedition to get you. Now I have to wipe out the sound before it reaches him." He dug a small hole in his floor, put salt in it, then some powder from a packet on his shelf, then some white chicken feathers. On top of that he poured a little rum. He sang a brief song, after which he filled in the hole with dirt. He was tired from his frantic exertions and was breathing hard. I said, "Grandfather, I am sorry. I did not know about not mentioning the name." He said, "Do not speak of it. It is you I am worried about. If they should ever come to this house they would look at me and say, 'What do we want with that old man? He can hardly walk.' And they would go away."

XI

All the things I had heard were swirling around in my mind, and I had trouble falling asleep. When at last I did, it was not happy sleeping. I had dark and frightening dreams. But they were not really dreams. I was lying there on Hector Soubré's sleeping mat and my eyes were closed, but everything that happened was very real. The first thing I remember was seeing my grandfather, Djalan. At first I was very happy, thinking, "Ah, he is still alive," but there was something strange about him. He hardly spoke and when he did it was in another language, though I understood everything he said. He seemed to look right through me as if I was not there and he was seeing something behind me. I wondered if he was angry with me for some reason, but he did not speak any angry words.

He said, "Dosu, let us go now to the funeral." I was frightened and asked him, "Grandfather, what funeral?" He said, "Why, the funeral of your father. He died last night." I said, "No, no, Grandfather, it must have been someone else!" He looked at me with a mournful face. He said, "How can I be mistaken? I have received the message. It is my son Golo who has died. He will be coming soon. I will be seeing him here Below the Water. But first the funeral must be carried out properly. Both of us must be there." A feeling of dread seized me. I did not know where I was or what was happening. Djalan said, "You living people do not understand anything. Dying is only traveling from one place to another. Today your father is there, tomorrow he will be here. But we must go to the funeral to make things easy for him." I said, "But Grandfather, where is 'here?'" He said, "Why, we are in Yzolé, Below the Water." I said, "Grandfather, it is too far to go. We cannot get there in time." He said, "You do not understand. Distance is only for the living." I said, "But am I not still alive?" He said, "Yes, but you are with me, and that changes everything. Now we are leaving."

I did not feel as if I were traveling anywhere, but instead of where I had been I was immediately at the house of my father and mother. Many people were gathered around the house, old people, young people, and children. The older ones were sitting here and there on benches, all looking very sorrowful, some talking in low voices, some saying nothing. Younger people were behaving as they always did at a good-time party, laughing and telling jokes, which I did not like, but that was the way it always was at death gatherings. Off to one side, under a large tree, young children were sitting on the ground and a samba was telling them stories.

I heard my mother's voice from inside the house, wailing to my father that he had left her alone in the world and that she would never be able to do all the things necessary to stay alive. But a few minutes later she came out with coffee for the people on the benches. When she saw me her wailing began all over again, and most of the old women joined in. When her crying stopped she said, "Dosu, go inside, your father is waiting for you." I went inside the house, which was very crowded. Everyone was doing something or calling out instructions. In the middle of the crowd my father was lying very quietly on his mat as if sleeping. I went to him and took his hand. I said, "Papa, I came as soon as I could." I heard my grandfather say over my shoulder, "He knows, he knows." I said, "Papa, you look very handsome in your fine clothes, just as if you were going to the city." I heard my aunt Cecile say, "Yes, just as if he were paying a visit to that Lorgina Labelle down there." I heard my grandfather Djalan reprove her. He said, "If you have nothing good to tell Jérémie, why did you come?" She went away and joined her friends outside the house.

When new guests arrived they came to my father's side and spoke to him. One old man touched my father's shoulder and said, "Jérémie, my good friend, why did you have to go? It would have been better if we were sitting at my house playing mayamba. You would win and I would get angry, then I would win and you would get angry, then we would drink some tafia and be happy. Who is going to sit with me now? Listen, Jérémie, when you get where you are going, don't forget to greet my parents and my sister for me." I asked the man, "Did my father hear you?" He said, "Yes, didn't you see him smile? Also, he moved his finger. Whenever I talk too much he moves his finger that way." Another man came to my father's side. He was someone I knew, named Ouvri Porte Pour Moin, Open the Door for Me. He said, "Jérémie, my old friend, you are an honorable man. Tell your family to return the hoe you borrowed from me. You will not need it in Yzolé where you are going. May your journey be a good one. Say bonjou' to my brothers when you get there. Do not forget me."

This went on all morning, until at last it was time for Kuku Cabrit to remove the guardian spirit from my father's head. He kneeled astride my father's body and grasped it by the shoulders. He said, "Jérémie, my friend, now the vodoun in your head must be liberated. Hevioso has served and protected you. He has made your life good, but he has to leave you now. You do not need him any more. Now you are going to Yzolé, Below the Water, to Ville au Camp. Let Hevioso go. Let him go. Let him go. Sit up, Jérémie, sit up, sit up!" My father had seemed very peaceful, but now his face became tense and he shuddered. Slowly he sat up on on his mat and his eyes opened. I had seen this before at the déssounin service for my grandfather, but still I was frightened that my father, who was dead, obeyed Kuku Cabrit's command. The two of them looked into each other's eyes. Kuku Cabrit said, "My good friend, now we will liberate Hevioso from your head so that he will leave you alone and not make you do things that will distress your family." He picked up the jar that was supposed to receive the spirit from my father's head.

Then something happened that startled even Kuku Cabrit. My father rose to his feet and began walking. The people who crowded the room were terrified and rushed out the door. Men were shouting and women were screaming. Kuku Cabrit called out, "No, no, my friend! Come back to your mat!" But my father walked slowly around the room as if he were searching for something or somebody. People who were still inside cowered against the walls. My father went up to one man who was cringing in a corner and pointed a finger at him. After that he returned to his mat and sat down. The man in the corner was trembling. He leaped through the door crazily and went running into the fields.

Kuku Cabrit said, "Ah! Ah! Now we know something!" He straddled my father's legs again and touched the jar to my father's forehead. My father's eyes closed and Kuku Cabrit helped him to lie down. Once more my father's face looked very peaceful. Kuku Cabrit took the jar outside and shattered it against a stone, liberating the vodoun Hevioso.

They wrapped my father's body in a sleeping mat, and again my mother began to cry out that she was being left alone with no one to care for her. The grave that had been dug was only a short distance away, but they did not carry my father's body directly there. First they took him to the spring so that he could refresh himself before his journey. After that they went to a tree sacred to Hevioso, and Kuku Cabrit spoke, saying, "Hevioso, great vodoun, Jérémie thanks you for everything you have done to protect him and his family. He says he will see you below the water." They carried my father to many such special places. But each time the trail crossed another trail they stopped and waited until Kuku Cabrit addressed the Master of the Crossroads and the Highway, asking for permission to continue on. Finally they reached the grave and placed my father's body in it. When the grave was filled with earth they put bowls of corn and millet at the head, and on top of the grave they placed his machete and his garden knife and his knapsack.

Everyone went back to the house after that, but I stayed by the grave because I had not had much time to be near my father. Kuku Cabrit came to get me, and I asked him what it meant when my father's corpse rose to its feet and pointed at the man in the corner of the room. He said, "Your father was accusing him. We have to perform some divinations to find out what he meant to tell us." While I was talking to Kuku Cabrit my grandfather Djalan appeared again. He said, "Now it is over for us. Do not worry. I will meet your father and take care of him." I suddenly felt as if the whole world was dark and without anything in it.

Then I found myself lying in the house of the old man Hector Soubré. He was sitting on the ground wiping my forehead with a rag. He seemed very concerned, but when he saw that I was awake he smiled. I tried to get up but I felt quite weak. He said, "No, no, do not get up yet. You have been on a journey." I said, "Papa, I have not been anywhere. I have been having some frightening dreams." He shook his head. "You have not been dreaming. You have been somewhere. What you saw was true." I said, "No, what I saw could not be true. I dreamed that I was at my father's funeral with my grandfather, Djalan. Have I not been here all this time in your house?"

Hector Soubré shook his head. "You have been here and you have been there. Whatever you saw, that is where you were." I said, "You gave me this mat to lie on, and I am still here. About my father's funeral, that was only a bad dream." Hector Soubré said, "My son, it was not a dream. Whatever you saw, it was the truth." He did not say anything for a while, then he went on, "Tell me about your grandfather, whom you called Djalan." I told him Djalan had died some time ago. He nodded his head. "Yes, that is the way it was. Your grandfather knew instantly when your father died. He came here to get you. He transported you to the funeral, and when it was finished he transported you back. In that place under the water, the dead know everything that is going on. Because your grandfather loved you he wanted you to be at the service so you could talk to your father. That is how it happened. Only the shell of your body was here. It was night, you went to sleep. In the morning you did not get up. You did not move. I thought perhaps you had died. But you were still breathing. I looked at the palms of your hands. They were blue. I looked at the soles of your feet. They were blue. I looked at your navel. It was blue. I knew then that you had gone on a journey, that someone from Below the Water had taken you somewhere. There was nothing to do but wait."

I said, "Papa, how long was I gone?" He said, "You were gone all day." That was how long I had been at the funeral service. I could hardly say anything because I was so downcast about the death of my father. I asked if my family knew I had been there, and Hector Soubré answered, "Yes, you were really there and everyone saw you." I said, "Thank you for taking care of me here in your house." He said, "No, do not thank me, give thanks to your grandfather Djalan." I said aloud, "Yes, Grandfather Djalan, thank you for coming for me." When I started to get to my feet, the old man stopped me. He said, "First there is something to be done." He opened a little packet and took out some red powder. He rubbed the powder on my hands and the soles of my feet and my navel. After that I was allowed to get up from the mat.

When I stood up I felt something heavy in my pocket. I discovered it to be my father's thunder stone, the one Hevioso had hurled at our habitation. Then I knew for certain that everything Hector Soubré had told me was the truth. But I began to worry about my mother. Now both Jean-Jacques and I were gone and there was no one to clear the brush and do other heavy work. I thought perhaps I should return instead of going on, so that my mother would have at least one son with her. My spirit became heavy and I could not decide what to do. I told Hector Soubré I was thinking of going back because my mother did not have anyone to help her. He asked if my father had belonged to any kind of a société, and I said no, but my brother Jean-Jacques belonged to the society called Habitation of the

Beautiful Pines. Hector Soubré told me not to worry then, because the society would do all my mother's heavy work until my brother or I returned.

I was much affected by my father's death. The one thing I remembered most vividly about the funeral service was my father getting to his feet and pointing at the man cringing in the corner of the room. What Kuku Cabrit said about it meant that the man had poisoned my father or sent an expedition against him. Perhaps Kuku Cabrit would solve it by divination before I returned home, but if not, I would have a grave responsibility to perform. I thought that maybe the man ran away merely because he was terrified by a corpse pointing at him, but I knew my father was a good man and would not accuse anyone unless there was a reason.

I said goodbye to Hector Soubré and again thanked him for everything he had done for me. I also said goodbye to his daughter Élizia and her husband. Élizia gave me some bread wrapped in a leaf, and her last words to me were, "Look out for Pied Coupé. Wear this wrist band, it may protect you." She gave me a wristband made of horsehair with some snake bones woven into it. I put it on and began my way up the mountain.

The trail was very faint, as though it were not used very much, and sometimes I could not see it at all. In late morning I stopped to eat some of the bread Élizia had given me, but I did not eat very much because I wanted it to last. Afterwards I noticed a mockingbird in the treetops. It went from one tree to another just ahead of me, stopping to see if I was following. People said that mockingbirds often did that to keep people on the right trail. I had heard that during the Revolution a mockingbird had helped Dessalines outflank a French army and destroy it. The mockingbird would fly in the air, then swoop down to where Dessalines was sitting on his horse and call out, "Go east, go east, go east," after which it would fly up and take another look. Then it would come down again and call, "Up the ravine, up the ravine, up the ravine," and Dessalines would take his troops up the ravine. In this way he was able to attack the French army from behind and win the battle. But the mockingbird that was accompanying me only made a few calls which didn't help in any way because I didn't understand what he was saying.

Late in the afternoon I reached the crest of the mountain. Though I could not see very much because of the dense pine groves, I knew I was no longer climbing, and at last when I emerged from the trees I was in a wide spreading grassland. In the distance the land dropped off, with clouds behind, and beyond them I could see a number of ridges. I wondered how many ridges I would still have to climb to get wherever I was going. Where would I ever find what I was looking for?

XII

That night I ate what was left of Élizia's bread and made a nest of grass next to a fallen pine. But a cold wind swept across the mountain and I shivered and could not sleep. I pictured a fire in my mind, thinking it might warm me, but it did not help and I had to get up and move around to keep from shaking. It must have been midnight when I heard the faint sound of singing in the distance. I thought, "There are people somewhere. Maybe they will give me a place to sleep," but it was hard to tell where the sound was coming from.

After a while the voices became louder, and I realized that the singers were coming in my direction. I peered in the starlight but could not see anything. Then, unexpectedly, a moving spark of light appeared in a hollow down below and the wind brought me the words of the song. I heard a single voice saying, "Go, go, you are only earth," and a number of voices answered, "Yes, we are going, we are only earth." As the voices came closer I saw a procession moving in single file, lighted by several torches. There was a long line of men, and behind them was a man dressed in the uniform of a general. He held a bullwhip which he cracked rhythmically in the air to keep time for the marchers. I wondered what kind of work party would be out here at this time of the night.

Though they were moving forward, the men were not walking in the usual way. They did not go from toe to heel, but merely slid their feet along the ground. They seemed to be looking in front of them but their eyes were closed. When they were very close I could make out what they were singing. The general called out commandingly in time to the cracking of the bull whip:

> Go, go, my zombies, you are only earth!
> Eh-yeh-ee-wa, listen to the bullwhip,
> Its name is Lambam of Ouanaminth,
> It is Lambam who knows how to cut skin,
> It is Lambam who knows how to pierce flesh!

And the long line of foot-sliding men chanted back in low, lifeless voices:

> Yes, Papa Lambam of Ouanaminth,
> We are going, we are going,
> Don't you see how we are trying to go?
> Do not cut our skin, Papa Lambam!
> Do not pierce our flesh, Papa Lambam,
> We are only earth! Eh-yeh-ee-wah!

Over and over they sang the words, first the general, then the procession of slowly moving men, and all the time the bullwhip was cracking in the air.

So then I knew. But what were they doing out here at midnight? Where did they come from and where were they going? I stood watching from behind a tree, so frightened that I could not move. Slowly, slowly, the procession passed. The torches grew fainter and at last disappeared. After that for a short while I heard faint singing, then there was nothing more. I took out my Hevioso thunder stone and held it in my hands. I called to Hevioso to protect me and tell me what to do. The stone was cold, but when it began to warm up I saw a small burst of flash lightning in the clear sky and decided that my plea to Hevioso had been heard.

I could not get out of my mind those pitiful men who called the bullwhip Papa Lambam of Ouanaminth. I went back to my grass nest and lay there the rest of the night without closing my eyes. Was Lambam some kind of vodoun? I had never heard of him. But I sensed that what I had seen had something to do with what I was looking for. In the morning I walked to the edge of the mountaintop, which ended in a steep cliff. Down below was a wide green valley and at the far end, small in the distance, I could see a group of thatched buildings and a wide stretch of gardens and cane fields. Somehow I knew that at last I was looking at Habitation Perdue. I was reluctant to go any further. I did not know what I was going to do now that I was here. For one thing, I could not find any trails that could take me down to the valley floor. And should I somehow get down there, what if I were to run into another procession such as the one I had already seen?

In the afternoon I lay on a warm rock and slept for a while. When I awoke, I looked again for a trail but did not find any. I remembered that the shuffling men with the torches had gone down somewhere, and so I turned and searched in another direction. Just as night was falling I found the place. My empty stomach was paining me. I had not had anything to eat since the evening before, but I was tired and weak and needed to rest. So I gathered grass again and made another nest in the brush. This time I fell into a deep sleep. I dreamed about Kuku Cabrit straddling the body of my dead father and commanding him to sit up and open his eyes. I also saw my brother walking about the room, shuffling his feet and moving slowly, singing "Lambam of Ouanaminth" over and over, and this terrified me greatly because he seemed to be one of the zombies I had seen the previous night.

When I awoke, the sun had already risen over the eastern ridge. For some reason I did not feel as hungry as the day before, though I hadn't eaten anything since then. But I needed water. There had been a heavy morning fog, however, and I was able to lick dew off the leaves of plants. I descended the mountainside and at a certain place discovered a trail which seemed to go down toward the valley. At one point I saw a goat skull and a human skull hanging from a tree branch, but I turned my face quickly so that I would not have to look at them because I knew they had some kind of magical force. After I passed, I heard them knocking together in the wind.

For a while after that I heard nothing. There were no bird or lizard sounds. Later on I sometimes heard the creaking of trees as they rubbed together in the breeze. The trail was well worn as if it were constantly used, and here and there I could see a footprint in the dust, but no living people were visible.

At one place the way became very steep, and I slipped on the wet clay and fell, striking my head on a rock. I did not feel well after that, and yearned for some water both to drink and to wash off my bleeding head. I did not find a spring anywhere. I came to a large pothole filled with muddy water. The water tasted very bad, but I swallowed some of it anyway. Unexpectedly, when the sun was beginning to go down, the trail became level and I saw a courtyard and a clean lime-covered house with a fresh straw roof. A young woman was pestling her mortar just outside the door. I approached her and asked, "Mademoiselle, may I have a little taste of water?" Even as miserable as I felt, I noticed that she was very beautiful. She gave me a gourd of water, then more until I had had enough. I sat on the ground and she went on pestling for a while without saying anything. Then she asked where I came from. I had learned by now not to tell everything I knew, and I answered, "From the south." She said, "Strangers don't usually use this trail." I said, "As it happened, I was up on top and couldn't find any water or anything to eat. I took the trail thinking I would find a house or village down here." She said, "Well, you have found my house." I said I was Dosu Bordeaux and asked her name. She said it was Belle Figi. It was a good name, because she did have a beautiful face. Her skin was smooth and copper-colored.

When she was through pestling she said, "I do not have a husband. You can have something to eat with me." She brought out a pot of Congo beans mixed with bits of beef and put it on her fire. I watched her without saying anything, admiring her face and body. I became more and more drawn to her, forgetting for the moment why I was there so far from home. When the food was ready we ate, and I kept looking at her eyes. My feelings were stirred. The sun dipped behind the western ridge and night came. In the faint light of the fire Belle Figi's eyes glowed, like a cat's. She lighted an oil lamp inside the house and rolled out her sleeping mat. Without her saying so I knew she was inviting me to share the mat with her. I forgot the miseries of my journey, thinking only that fortune was good to me. We lay together and after a while we slept.

I cannot say how late in the night it was when I became aware of Belle Figi's heavy breathing. Rattling, disagreeable sounds were coming from her throat. I touched her body. It did not feel smooth and soft as it had earlier, but gnarled and leathery. Her face was turned away and I could not see it clearly in the dim light of the oil lamp, but her hair seemed grey rather than black. I became uneasy. I got up cautiously so as not to disturb her. I brought the lamp close to her face, and what I saw was not the beautiful Belle Figi but an old woman with deep wrinkles, only two teeth in the front of her mouth, yellowish white hair, and a running sore on her cheek. I pulled her coverlet back and saw that her body had no flesh on it, only bones and rough, wrinkled skin. What frightened me most was the slit that ran from her throat down between her shrivelled breasts to the bottom of her belly, because it told me that she was some kind of a lougaro who had gone out of her body, perhaps in the form of an animal, to prey on human beings. I frantically hung the oil lamp back on its hook, took my knapsack and other belongings, and went out of the house as silently as I could. There was no moon, only starlight, and it was difficult to see the trail that descended into the valley. I stumbled and fell several times and cut my knees on the rocks, but I kept walking until daylight came.

Recollections of my night with Belle Figi continued to agitate me, but gradually I began to feel a little better. I discovered that I didn't have all my belongings with me, having lost some of them on the trail or left them behind at the lougaro woman's house. I was very upset to find that my thunder stone was missing, but I could not go back for it no matter how great the loss.

Down below I could now see part of the valley floor and some signs of cultivation. Suddenly I realized that after my long hard journey I was about to arrive at Habitation Perdue. I didn't have any idea of what I was going to do next, but I was certain that somewhere in the valley I would find my brother. I can't say why I knew it, but it was almost as if there was a wind blowing from him, saying, "Dosu, here I am." I felt the world around me to be very strange. Nothing was really the way it looked. People, animals, birds, even rocks and trees were hostile and malevolent. I felt very alone, and couldn't even remember the faces of the people I knew back at Dleau Frète. I sat sharpening my machete on a stone, wondering about how I ought to start looking for Jean-Jacques. Then I realized that since I knew nothing at all about what the Habitation was like, I could not make a plan. I would just have to go ahead. Whatever would happen would happen.

But I was very hungry and felt weak. As I continued down the trail I looked for something to eat. At one place there were some mango trees, but the fruit was small not ripe. Nevertheless I tried knocking some of them down by throwing stones. It was good fortune, after a while, to hit one of them and it fell. I skinned it with my machete, but it was tasteless and too hard to chew. Then I heard an old man's voice from above saying, "Who is down there disturbing my mangoes?" I answered, "It is I, Dosu Bordeaux. Excuse me for disturbing your mangoes, but I am very hungry." No one replied but I thought I could see a grinning black face among the leaves. The leaves moved in the breeze and the face disappeared. I left the mango grove quickly, wondering what kind of tree spirit had spoken to me.

At last the ground flattened out and I was on the floor of the valley. My trail joined a road with deep ruts where two-wheel cane carts had traveled, but I did not see the hoofprints of any oxen. After going along the road for a while I heard a loud voice and the cracking of an ox whip. I quickly hid in the brush and waited. Very soon a loaded cane cart appeared with a man sitting on top of the cane. He was cracking his whip and shouting over and over, "Allez! Allez!" When the cart came closer I could see that there were no oxen in front. Instead of the oxen were eight men, four pairs of two, and each pair was yoked together with a wooden neck yoke. Never before had I seen or heard of such a thing. As the cart approached the place where I was hiding I saw that the men pulling it were not wearing ordinary clothes, but long shirts made of banana leaves held to their waists by ropes. They were not talking, only breathing hard, their eyes fixed on the ground.

The driver suddenly called out for them to stop. He turned his head this way and that, sniffing the air. I pressed as close to the ground as I could and held my breath. At last he cracked his whip and called out, "Allez! Allez!" and the cart began to move again. I raised my head a little to look again at the men who were doing the pulling, wondering if Jean-Jacques might be among them. I could not see their faces very well, but I didn't see anyone who might have been my brother or his friend André. In fact, most of the men looked very much alike, not only because of the way they were dressed but because of the dead stare with which they were looking at the ground. I knew without being told that all of those men were zombies, and began to wonder whether this was the way my brother would look if I ever found him.

After the cart was out of sight I continued along the road until I heard another cart coming. Again I hid in the brush. This second cart was pulled by women, and a woman driver was sitting up above on top of the cane. The women also wore long banana-leaf shirts, or maybe you could call them dresses, tied around their waists with ropes, and they also were looking at the dusty road with dead eyes. I suddenly became very fearful and stayed a long time in the brush where I was hiding.

I decided not to follow the road any more, as it was too dangerous. Instead, I went wherever there were no trails or signs of people, regardless of direction. Sometimes I was going north, sometimes south, and my whole purpose was just not to be seen. I kept wandering this way until darkness came, and then I climbed into a large tree and found a place to crouch on a heavy limb. I could not sleep because of the cold, but I stayed there shivering all night. When the sun rose I came down, but I did not know which way to go. I did not want to go anywhere for fear of encountering more zombies or, worse yet, any zombie drivers.

Ever since leaving home I had had only one thought in my mind, to get to Habitation Perdue, and I had been willing to suffer any kind of hardship and risk any kind of encounter on the way, but now that I was here I felt totally helpless and abandoned. I had no plan whatever about what I should do next, only that I should not be discovered. I looked back at the steep mountainside I had descended. I understood for the first time that those who had urged me not to attempt my journey were right, and considered whether under cover of the next darkness I should turn and go back.

I began walking aimlessly, not to get to any particular destination but only to warm my chilled body. Whenever I heard human sounds I turned away from them. I did not want to hear anything but silence. Sometimes I heard the cries of birds and yearned to hear the call of a mockingbird who could tell me "go this way" or "go that way," but there were no mockingbirds. Once I saw a tiny hummingbird, a negesse mambo, feeding at a red blossom. I stood still, hoping that the bird would give me some kind of a sign as to where I should go, but almost instantly it darted away and was gone. I kept looking for a coco palm, hoping to find a ripe coconut and get something to drink from it, but up here in these mountains there seemed to be no palms. I was feeling weak from hunger, but more than anything else I needed something to drink. Once I found a muddy patch of earth where rainwater had settled. I dug into it with my fingers but didn't find any water below. Then when I was feeling very hopeless I heard the faint sound of running water and found a small brook running between two tall pines. I buried my face in the water and drank, and after that I lay on my back and rested on a warm flat rock.

The air was very silent, but after a while I began to hear something beneath the silence, the sounds of machetes cutting into stalks of cane, and sometimes the crack of a stalk being broken. I strained for the sound of voices, but it was a while before I heard a faint "Allez! Allez!" So I knew there were cane-cutters at work out there somewhere. The water had given me heart, and I decided to bring my frantic running in circles to an end. I made my way cautiously toward where I believed the canefield to be, but echoes from the surrounding mountains made the direction uncertain. Eventually I came to a rocky mound, and when I reached the top all the sights and sounds became clear. Cane was growing thickly in a flat stretch of plain. I could see several cane carts standing nearby, and even though they were small in the distance I observed that men, women, and children were working with machetes and loading the carts. Again I noticed that the carts had no oxen harnessed to them.

I crept through the underbrush as close as I dared. The workers moved slowly, never stopping to rest. I could see by their motions that they were zombie slaves. One man's hat fell off as he bent over, but he made no effort to retrieve it. Another was wearing a single sandal. Some were naked, their banana-leaf shirts having fallen off. Several drivers marched from one end of the field to the other, cracking their ox whips and shouting "Allez!" if they saw any of the workers slowing down. The workers themselves never turned their heads or spoke to one another. It was the same with the children as with the older people. One old man gradually stopped moving. He simply stood like a post in the ground, his arms hanging at his sides. A nearby driver cracked his whip, but still the old man was motionless. The driver poked at him with a stick. The machete dropped from the old man's hand and he fell stiffly into the cane stubble. The driver was irritated and angry. He said, "Ah! Li mort!!" He ordered some of the zombie workers to dig a hole. With clumsy movements they dug a shallow grave there in the canefield with picks, pushed the corpse into it and covered it over. Then they went on cutting cane. This scene shocked me a great deal. It was not the way humans were meant to be buried, with regret and respect. There was no mourning, no wailing. No one said, "Goodbye, my friend." The other zombies did not even seem to notice that one of them had disappeared. I wondered about the spirit that had once occupied the old man's head. Was it also under the ground now, or had it departed long ago?

My hunger was making me feel ill, and I crawled back into the dense brush and began searching for anything that might be edible. I found a wild carrot and tried to pull it from the ground, but the stem broke and I had to dig it out with a stick. It did not taste very good raw, but I forced it down. I also ate some ants and grasshoppers, but they did not help my hunger. I had heard of people eating plain earth when they were starving, and I was about to do the same thing when I saw a crippled bird that had fallen from a tree. I quickly captured it, killed it, and ate the flesh, of which there was not very much.

By this time it was late afternoon. Dark clouds appeared over the western mountain ridge. There was thunder and lightning and rain began to fall, and I took refuge in a grove of pines. They did not protect me from the downpour at all, and I might as well have been out in the open. But I noticed that one of the taller pines began to glow, particularly around the top, and I wondered if it might be some kind of sign. Then there was a brilliant flash and a loud roar, and I saw a line of fire running down the whole length of the tree trunk. The rain stopped almost as suddenly as it had begun and the day became bright again.

The tree that had been struck by lightning was still smoldering and some of its branches had fallen to the ground. I was grateful that I had not taken shelter there. It came to my mind that the vodoun Hevioso was one of my protectors. Somewhere near the tree there had to be the thunder stone he had thrown and I began at once to look for it. I searched all afternoon but found nothing. When night came I gathered a pile of brush to sleep on. Hunger pained my stomach, but I slept, and in the morning I continued my searching. At last I gave up and started walking. I had gone no more than fifty steps when I found the thunder stone partially buried in the ground. I cleaned it off and saw that it was almost identical to the one I had left behind in the house of Belle Figi, the lougaro. I was very happy. I danced around, singing,

Hevioso, Papa, thank you!
Papa Hevioso, my vodoun,
Thank you for what you have given me!
Never again will I lose the stone!
You have given me courage!
Now I will find my brother Jean-Jacques!

In my pocket I still had the small fragment of iron given to me by Kuku Cabrit, and on my wrist I was still wearing the horsehair wrist band given to me by Élizia to protect me from Pied Coupé, the tree demon with one leg. I felt very light-hearted, and for a while I forgot that I was hungry. When I looked down at the valley from the mountainside I had the impression that most of the activities and buildings, indeed the whole plantation, were located in the middle, and it now came to me that the first thing I ought to do was to explore around the outer edges to get a better idea of everything. This is what I did, clinging to the thick brush as much as possible. Now and then I crossed a small trail, and once a rutted road for cane carts. It was on the road that I found a stalk of cane, and I was sure that one of my protective vodouns had caused it to fall there. I chewed on the cane as I walked. It gave me strength and at the same time quenched my thirst.

When I reached the far side of the valley I still had not seen anything helpful. Just as the light was beginning to fade I came to a small rock outcropping with a cave-like opening and decided to remain there for the night. Although the ground inside was damp I lay down and quickly fell asleep. I cannot say how long I had been sleeping when I was awakened by a burning pine torch over my head. I jumped to my feet in panic, but heard a voice saying, "Doucement, doucement!" Then I saw a hand holding the torch and, behind it, a bearded man in a banana-leaf shirt. He was looking at me closely. He said, "Who are you? You do not belong here." I answered anxiously, "No, no, I was just on my way to a certain place and I came into the cave to sleep." He asked, "You don't live on the Habitation?" I said, "No, it is just as I told you. My name is Dosu Bordeaux.

I come from the east." He sat down and was silent. I said, "You, m'sieu, I think you must be one—you must be one of them."

He did not answer directly. He said, "Why are you here?" I did not know if it was safe to tell him anything. He said, "Do not worry too much, you can trust me." I said, "Well, I am looking for someone. I heard he might be here." He shook his head. "What will you do if you find him? What if they find you first?" All I could say was "Ahhh!" As my eyes became accustomed to the torchlight I saw that the man was carrying a calabash. And while I was contemplating what my fate would be if I were caught, he got down on his hands and knees and crawled through a small hole in the back of the cave. When he returned, his calabash was full of water. I asked if there was a spring back there. He let me sip from his calabash. The water was salty. He stuck his torch in a crack in the rocks and sat down.

In a little while he spoke again, saying, "So you are a stranger from the east?" I said, "Yes, my family lives in the mountains above Dleau Frète." He said, "I never heard of it. Who are you looking for?" I said, "My younger brother and his friend." He asked, "How do you know he is at Habitation Perdue?"I said, "It was made known to me. It was told in a dream, and my vodouns verified it. Also, when I was on top of the mountain I heard his voice in the breeze." He said, "Which vodouns are you speaking about?" I said, "Ogoun inhabits my head, and Hevioso is the master of our house." He answered, "You are fortunate. But even the vodouns do not like to interfere with things at Habitation Perdue. Only Gèdé of the Graveyard likes it here. There is a big shrine for him on the other side of the canefields. Sometimes the zombie masters make a service for him." I answered, "But Hevioso cannot be afraid of anything. He hurls thunder stones from the sky. And Ogoun is a great warrior."

We sat silently for a while. Then I asked him his name. "He said, "We do not use our own names here. Some of us are called by numbers. Others are given names no one understands." I said, "But you once had a name, and you came from somewhere." He said, "Most of the people here do not remember their names. They do not remember anything." I said, "You do not seem to be like those others." He did not answer immediately, but finally he said, "I am finding my way back, little by little." I asked many questions, some of which he did not answer. I asked how it was possible for a zombie to regain his normal state of living. He said there were several ways, but most of the zombies were too nearly dead to even think about them. I began to ponder why this man would come to this remote place for his water. Suddenly I understood. The water was salty! I told him my thoughts. He said, "Yes, I drink it and I bring some back for two of my friends." He looked at me menacingly, saying, "If you give my secret away I will kill you!" I said hurriedly, "Yes, yes, if I ever speak of it to anyone you may kill me." I could see he regretted having spoken of the salt water. He said, "It is too great a risk. Perhaps I will kill you now."

I spoke urgently, saying, "There is no need for it. I know no one here. All I want is my brother and his friend. I am hiding out here in the brush because I don't want to meet any of the zombie masters. When I find my brother and his friend we will go away as swiftly as possible. I need to get home to take care of my mother's habitation. While I was on my journey my father died. My mother has no one to bring her wood and take care of the crops. Before coming here I never heard of Habitation Perdue. I would not be here at all except for the help of certain people who have deep knowledge. I had many dangerous experiences on the way. When I first saw the valley I wanted to turn back at once. But now I am here, and as soon as I find Jean-Jacques I will go. There is no reason to kill me."

The look on his face softened. He said, "There are four hundred and forty zombie slaves here on the Habitation. Which one is your brother? How are you going to know him if you see him? He will not look like he did before he disappeared. We all look alike, as if we were made of clay. If you call his name he will hear nothing. He cannot converse. If you say, 'My name is Dosu,' it will mean nothing to him. And if you ever find him, will you carry him home on your back?"

I said, "M'sieu, I heard you say there are several ways for a zombie to regain his normal state of life. I know about the salt.

I have heard many people speak of it." He said, "Yes, the bocor who brought your brother to his present condition could do it by preparing special medicines. But there are no bocors here. They all sold their victims to the Habitation and went away. Every bocor has his own methods. Some of them use a powder made of one hundred and one ingredients. Some have lotions that they rub into the skin. Some perform rituals, but no two rituals are alike. Some use candles made from the fat of dead human beings. One bocor came here to reclaim one of his victims. He had himself buried with the victim in a shallow grave, and shortly afterwards they emerged, the zombie completely cured. No one knows how it was done. And there is another thing. If the bocor's treatment does not succeed, the zombie dies and quickly crumbles into dust. There is only one thing left to us—salt, if we can get it. Put some salt into a zombie's mouth and he regains consciousness. But he may not be as he was before. He may be a madman."

I said, "But you, m'sieu, it is obvious that you have recovered." He answered, "I was sent out by my master to perform some work. I found this cave. I entered and found the salt spring. I was thirsty and drank. I felt myself changing. I drank again and began to understand what was happening. So I come here for water whenever I can and bring a calabash of it back to my two friends. Little by little they also are becoming their normal selves. But we all must behave as though we are still complete zombies. Some day we will get away." But again he began to look concerned and hostile as if he had said too much and regretted it. I thought perhaps I should get out of the cave as quickly as possible, but he was between me and the entrance. I said, "If I knew how to help you I would. And perhaps you could help me find my brother Jean-Jacques and his friend André." He said, "Never mind. I see you have a good heart. You won't do anything wrong. You were a fool to come here, but maybe your vodouns will protect you." Without any more conversation he turned and crawled out of the cave with his torch and his calabash of water. It was then I noticed for the first time that he had a pattern of scars on his legs, several small crosses on each calf that reminded me of the tribal marks some of the old people had on their bodies. Kuku Cabrit had a different kind of mark, on his shoulder, and an old woman of Dleau Frète had three straight lines on her forehead.

XIII

When morning came I continued walking around the outer edge of the valley. Occasionally I heard distant voices from the area of the fields and the buildings, but gradually came to feel that I was doing nothing useful. Suddenly I was startled by the sound of a drum and a conch horn immediately ahead, and I heard a hoarse voice calling, "Raise your hoe! Down with it! Up, down! Up, down!" I flattened myself against the ground and crawled slowly forward. Soon I saw a coumbite, a work party, tilling the ground. There were about thirty men, all clothed in banana leaves, in a long line, and a driver behind them with an ox whip. At the word "up," they raised their hoes above their heads in unison, and at the word "down," they brought their hoes down on the earth. One worker looked very much like the next one. I realized something I had never been told. None of them had any character. Each one seemed just like the others in every way, except that some were young and some were old. The way they stood was the same, the way they looked at the ground was the same, the way they moved their hoes was the same. If one of them was not in unison, the driver struck him with the ox whip.

I was very much upset by the sight of all these men without any character, nothing to distinguish one from another. I began to remember some of the things my father had told me about zombies, whom he often referred to as zombwiries. He said that when a bocor made a zombie the first thing he did was to remove his victim's head spirit. If he did not do this, the head spirit would revive the person and prevent the bocor from taking control. To keep the head spirits from regaining control, the bocors would transfer them and imprison them in jugs or jars. So all those men working in front of me with hoes were nothing but empty shells, and their maît' têtes were miles away in various bocors' establishments. I was very agitated by what I saw. Also, I wondered how giving them salt could restore them. It occurred to me that if all the jars in which the maît' têtes were held could be found, one need only break the jars and release them. But who could ever find those jars, hidden in so many different places? They probably were all buried in the ground.

I noticed several large grey pigs rooting nearby. Sometimes they stopped and sniffed the air. They began looking in my direction and moving toward me. I am not certain whether it was the Hevioso stone in my pocket that spoke or whether it was a voice in the breeze, but I heard the words, "The grey pigs are watchdogs searching for intruders." I fled at once into the deep brush, running as fast as I could and getting badly scratched by briars. I did not stop running until I was exhausted. I wished I was back at my small cove with the spring, but there was no chance of reaching it before dark, even if I could find it again. So I rested until I had recovered a little and then began to walk again.

As soon as the setting sun reached the western ridge, darkness came quickly, and I looked here and there for a place to sleep. My stomach was crying for food, and I blamed myself for not finding something to eat while there was still daylight. I appealed to Ogoun to help me. I placed my hand in my pocket, touched the piece of iron Kuku Cabrit had given me and sang softly:

Ogoun oh, I am in trouble!
Papa Ogoun, help me!

Ogoun, I am one of your children!
Ogoun, do not neglect your child!

Nothing happened to indicate Ogoun had heard me, and I was discouraged. Then I happened to remember those mystic words Kuku Cabrit had given me, and I spoke them as forcefully as I could:

Agoé! Agola! Agochi!

There was a burst of light, and suddenly I was on my feet dancing. I did not decide to dance. My body was moving according to its own will. For a moment I seemed to see my Grandfather Djalan carrying a musket, and the two of us were dancing together. He put gunpowder on my tongue and fire came out of my mouth. I had my machete in my hand and was striking out with it in all directions. I was not dancing any more, I was in some kind of battle. There were flashes of light all around. I saw Ogoun himself riding by on a white horse, a saber in each hand. Many things happened. I cannot remember most of them. Everything faded away and I fell unconscious.

I did not awaken until daylight. I was lying sprawled on the ground, my machete in my hand. For a while I did not try to move, because it was as if a heavy weight were holding me down. Gradually the weight disappeared. I arose and found myself scratched and bleeding from falling and thrashing in the brush. I knew that I had been mounted by Ogoun. While my vodoun had been riding me I had slashed down branches from the trees with my machete. On one of them I found a large ripe mango, even though I did not see any mango trees nearby. I thanked Ogoun, and sang:

Ogoun Papa, I am your grateful child!
Papa Ogoun, thank you for keeping me alive!

I ate the mango and felt much stronger. Also, I was not afraid any more. I knew that Ogoun was watching over me, and that Hevioso also was nearby.

I decided to find my way back to the cave in the hope of

meeting once more with the man who came there for salt water. I found the cave more easily than I expected, and as there was still a little daylight I gathered some leaves and small branches to sleep on. While I was sitting quietly a small zagouti wandered in, but when it saw me it ran out quickly. On the chance that it would come back, for whatever reason, I found a heavy stick and trimmed it with my machete. A little later the zagouti reappeared and I killed it with my stick. That night I had raw zagouti meat to eat. I did not like raw meat, but I had no choice.

The next day I wandered carefully toward the canefields. I hadn't gone far before I came to a shrine for Gèdé, the graveyard vodoun. A heavy wooden cross stood in a pile of stones, and a black hat was sitting on the top. Two skulls hung from the ends of the crossbar, and others were piled around the base. Leaning against the base of the cross were a shovel and a mattock used for digging graves. On a flat altar made of dried mud were a number of red clay jugs used to house spirits taken from people's heads when they died, and also several empty rum bottles. White skulls were painted on some of the flat rocks, all of them speckled with black spots which meant smallpox. A man clothed in a banana-leaf shirt moved listlessly on the far side of the shrine sweeping the ground of debris. His eyes were barely open, and there was no exertion in his movements, only a repetition of sweeping motions.

I had an impulse to speak with him, and after making sure no one else was nearby I approached him and said, "Bon soir, Papa." He did not seem to be aware that I was there. He just went on sweeping. It was the first time I had tried to converse with a zombie, but it was like talking to an empty basket. I tried to think of some way of making my presence known. I reached out and took the broom from him. He did not resist but continued moving his hands from side to side as if he still held the broom handle. He did not open his eyes or turn his head. I put the broom back in his hands and he went on working. I remembered some of the words I had heard the zombie drivers use, and I said sharply, "Rèté!" He stopped moving. I said, "Allez!" and he resumed his lethargic sweeping, never once looking at me.

When I heard voices in the distance I ran quickly into the dense brush, finding a place from which I could still see the shrine. Four men appeared, carrying a long sack by its corners. From their vitality and their clothing I could tell that they were not zombies. They dropped their sack and pulled a corpse from it. The nostrils and ears of the body were stuffed with cotton, and a band of cloth over its head held the chin in place so that the mouth would not open. They put the corpse on the ground in front of the shrine and left. The sweeper went on sweeping. Though I had been very courageous up to this moment I was now frightened and fled back to my cave. Someone was inside sitting on the grass and brush I used as my sleeping mat. I was startled, but relieved to see it was the man who came there to get water from the spring.

He did not speak immediately, and so I told him what I had just seen at the Gèdé shrine. He said, "Yes, that is why I am here. The corpse you saw was one of my friends to whom I have been bringing salt water. He made a mistake and revealed somehow that he was recuperating. They gave him zombie poison and he fell unconscious, just as you saw him. Tonight they are going to bury him in front of the shrine, try to remove the vodoun from his head, and revive him in the same condition as he was previously. Now, soon, they will be calling on the grey pigs to do their work and I will be in great danger."

I said, "M'sieu, I don't understand about the grey pigs." He said, "These grey pigs are like baka. They have the ability to tell by smell who is a zombie and who is not. The drivers put them on leashes and take them here and there. If a grey pig smells someone who is only pretending to be a zombie they will attack him. The drivers may pull them off or let them go, and if they let them go the pigs will kill and eat the person. If they do not find their victims in the fields or the sleeping quarters, the pigs are turned loose in the brush. Escape is very difficult. I will go back tonight with one more calabash of salt water, but then I think my other friend and I must try to get away quickly. You may come with us because your chances here are very bad and you are in great danger."

For a while I sat quietly, thinking only of Jean-Jacques and

André. The man said, "I found your brother and have been giving him salt water. He has recovered a little, but not completely. I will give him more salt water tonight. If he is sufficiently conscious and alert, I will try to bring him along. I do not know if his friend André is here any more. I could not find him, and Jean-Jacques could not tell me anything useful. Perhaps André is totally dead. Perhaps he was eaten by the grey pigs."

I said, "M'sieu, I am grateful to you. I do not even know your name, but when I get home we will perform a grand service in your honor." He said, "Here I am called by the number Eighty-Seven, but my real name is Émise Dubois. Now we are a société of four if your brother is strong enough to come. However it is too soon to know whether we can escape from the valley. The grey pigs are formidable." He took his calabash back to the spring and filled it. When he returned he said, "I will come back tomorrow about midnight with my friend Antoine. If your brother is fit enough I will bring him also, but I can't say for certain. It will depend on his strength and his state of mind. We will replenish our water and after that we will go. As soon as it is light tomorrow morning start gathering citronelle grass, as much as you can, and tie it in bundles." He left the cave with his calabash. I sat for a long while. I was full of joy that Émise had found Jean-Jacques and given him salt water to drink.

In the morning just as light began to glow over the eastern ridge I went out in search of citronelle grass. At first I found only a little here and there, but I came to a place where there was a great expanse of it. I cut with great energy, even though I was beginning to feel weak again for lack of food. Before the day ended I had six tied bundles of citronelle. All I had to eat were some roots that I dug from the ground with my machete. I brought my citronelle to the cave and waited. Darkness fell. Sometimes I came out and looked at the sky to see the time. The stars seemed to move very slowly. I listened intently to all the faint sounds floating in the night—tree frogs, an owl now and then, and night lizards. My hearing became very sharp. Finally I heard something making its way through the brush, and a moment later saw a spark of light that I knew was Émise Dubois' pine torch. When the light was close to the cave I could see that there were only two men, not three, and my heart turned heavy. I was certain that Jean-Jacques had been left behind. Despite everything Émise had told me, I resolved that I would not leave without my brother.

The two men entered the cave. One of course was Émise. And the other? I cannot describe how jubilant I was to see Jean-Jacques. We embraced without saying anything. Instead of the customary banana-leaf shirt, Jean-Jacques was wearing ragged pants held to his waist by a length of sisal twine. I could see, even in the dim light, that he was very emaciated. Then I turned to Émise, who had not said a word. I asked, "Where is your friend?" He looked away. "He was sniffed out by the grey pigs and taken somewhere. I don't know what the zombie masters are going to do with him. They spoke of pounding his head in a mortar. I could not do anything. I threw away my banana-leaf shirt and put this cloth around me. I stole a large packet of pepper from the masters' store room, took my cane knife, and left at once."

None of us spoke for a few minutes. Finally Émise went to the spring and drank. He told Jean-Jacques to do the same, but he would not allow me to drink, saying, "The salt is not good for you. From this moment we will all drink fresh water. Now we must go. I am sure they have already turned the grey pigs loose to track us." He extinguished his torch and led us out of the cave. We traveled by starlight, Émise in front, Jean-Jacques in the middle, and I behind. I could not see any trail, but Émise seemed to know where he was going. He opened the packet of pepper, which he sprinkled on the ground. Jean-Jacques and I scattered citronelle grass here and there, as Émise instructed us to do. We did not make any conversation, devoting all our energy to ascending the steep slope, often scraping our feet against sharp rocks and dislodging small stones that rolled downward behind us.

After much climbing we came to a flat place and stopped there to rest and catch our breath. I asked Émise about the purpose of the pepper and citronelle. He said, "The citronelle absorbs the scent, making it difficult for the grey pigs to smell our footsteps. If they sniff some of the pepper it is hard for them to smell anything else. Perhaps they will become muddled and stop their chase altogether. I don't know for sure, but they say it is so." I asked, "Is this the same side of the valley where I entered?" He said, "No, that is the easy slope over there. They will look for us on that side first." I asked what was beyond the mountain we were climbing and he said, "Only the vodouns and the ancestors know. Maybe there is another Habitation Perdue over there." I became agitated at the thought. After only a brief time we were on our way again, and we did not stop until the sun came up. We found a small pine grove and decided to stop there to rest. Émise lay down on some pine needles and fell asleep instantly.

For the first time Jean-Jacques and I had a chance to talk. Both of us were exhausted, but we wanted to know everything about each other. He wanted to know about his wife and child, then about our mother and father. I told him his wife and child were well when I last saw them, and that our mother also was well. It was hard to tell him about the death of our father, but I recounted how grandfather Djalan came to me from Yzolé Below the Water and took me to our father's death services. At first he did not want to believe me, saying it was only a dream, but I recounted every detail, including having the Hevioso stone in my possession when I awoke. Jean-Jacques was very downcast. I told him briefly about my journey to find him, passing over many small things because I knew he was deeply saddened by our father's death.

At last I asked, "Jean-Jacques, what happened to you? How did you get here?" He said, "Most of it I cannot remember. André and I went to Dleau Frète for seed, but there wasn't any to be found in the market. Someone told us that a certain man named Justin might have some, and we started up the trail to his house. Before we got there an old man on the road advised us to leave the trail we were on and take a side trail. This was what we did." I interrupted him, asking, "Was he lame and using a crotch cane?" Jean-Jacques said yes, it was that way. I said, "Ai! He was the same one that turned me off the trail! Legba, Master of the Highway! Did you come to a place where you heard voices but saw no people?" He said, "Yes, that is the way it was. We crossed a deep gully and came to a small house. There was a man sitting in the doorway and we asked him for a gourd of water. He went inside to get water from a large canarie and brought a gourd to each of us. After drinking I did not feel so well, and my eyesight became blurred. André also felt sick. We decided to continue our way but could not get up from where we were sitting.

"The man said, 'Do not worry about it. It happens sometimes.' He went back into his house and returned with a packet of red powder which he sprinkled on our heads. He said, 'In a moment everything will be all right.' But it was not all right. When I tried to speak, it was very difficult. Then my hearing became dim. The man spoke to us, but it was as if he was far away. He sprinkled something else on us and forced some kind of liquid into our mouths from a bottle. I cannot describe it to you, Dosu, except by saying I felt dead—dead but not quite dead. I could see the man moving about but only faintly. I remember other men coming and digging a wide grave behind the house. André and I were laid in it, our nostrils and ears were stuffed with cotton, and then we were covered with earth.

"How long we were there I cannot tell. Perhaps a few moments, perhaps a day or more. After a while there were digging sounds and we were dragged out. It was night. Several torches were burning nearby. I remember that the man had a sharp piece of bamboo which he dipped into a bowl and then scratched across my forehead. He told André and me to rise. We stood up, but it was as if life had gone out of our bodies. Whatever he commanded we did. If he said, 'Walk,' we walked. If he said 'Stop,' we stopped. We could not do anything unless he commanded us. People crowded in a circle around us and sang a song something like 'Wye wye, my zombies! You are only earth!' He walked us some distance away and tied us to a tree. It did not seem to matter that we couldn't sit or lie down. We were there all the next day. When night came he sprinkled more powder on us, tied us wrist to wrist and led us away. We were very docile, doing anything he told us to do. We came to a place where a woman and a boy were tied to a tree. He fastened their wrists to ours, and marched us every night along a mountain trail. I could not remember my name or where I came from. It was just endless walking. I don't know how long it took, but eventually I found myself at Habitation Perdue. I remember that a fat man named Gros Ventre came to look at us. He poked my stomach many times with the end of his walking stick. After that, I do not remember very much except hoeing or cutting cane."

Émise awoke and stood up, saying, "Let us keep going. We will not be safe until we cross the ridge." I said, "Yes, you are the one who leads and we will do whatever you say. But I need to know something. My brother was 'only earth.' How did you identify him, since he could hardly speak and did not even remember his name?" Émise replied, "I used the passage d'alliance." I said, "You must pardon me, but I do not really understand such things." He said, "It is done with a wari bean. The bean is pierced and tied to one end of a cord. The other end of the cord is fastened to a green twig cut from a calbasse tree. If you tell the wari bean that you are searching for a particular thing it will help you. I spoke these words to it: 'Wari bean, whose ancestor came with us from Guinée, give me your help. There is a man here named Jean-Jacques Bordeaux whom I must find quickly. In the name of the vodouns and the nations of Guinée, point him out for me because he is unable to speak for himself.' The old men I did not bother with, but each time I saw a young man about your age I held the wari bean over his head. Forty or fifty times I did this, but nothing happened. When I tried with Jean-Jacques the wari bean began to move, back and forth, back and forth, then around and around in a circle. In this way I found him, and after I gave your brother salt water to drink he was able to tell me from his own mouth who he was. I searched for André in the same way but could not find him. Now we must not waste any more time talking. Let us go."

So we continued our climbing, and in the daylight I could see that the mountainside was very steep. Everything we did seemed difficult because we had had so little rest. It was said that zombies could go for days without sleeping, but Jean-Jacques and Émise were no longer zombies. I was very thirsty and hungry but did not want to complain. We were all very happy when we found a pool of water at the bottom of a small waterfall. We stopped there, drank and washed our badly scraped legs and feet. I was in no hurry to leave but Émise urged us on. We did as he commanded. At mid-day we reached the ridge. For the first time I looked back into the valley. The canefields and buildings seemed tiny in the distance, and it was hard to imagine that there were people down there. There were pine groves on the ridge and it was not difficult to find a secluded spot to lie down. I wanted to ask Jean-Jacques many questions but almost immediately fell asleep. Jean-Jacques and Émise also slept.

I don't know how much time passed, but when I opened my eyes I saw an old man standing nearby watching us. I jumped to my feet and called for Émise and my brother to wake up. The old man continued to stare at us without speaking. He had a light complexion and long straight hair. He wore only a crude shirt and a loincloth. I said, "Bon soir, Papa," but though he looked directly at me he did not answer. I thought that perhaps he was some kind of baka, but Émise said, "Do not be concerned. He is only a Taino." Neither Jean-Jacques nor I knew anything about Tainos. Émise explained, "Tainos are another race, neither black nor white. They lived here before our people arrived from Guinée. Once they were everywhere on the island." Émise tried to speak with the old man, who only shook his head. He said, "Perhaps he is deaf or doesn't understand us." I still thought he might be some kind of baka who had taken a human form.

The old man turned away for a moment and motioned to someone behind him. Suddenly six more Taino men, most of them young, emerged from behind trees. One had a musket, but the others had spears which they held poised above their heads pointing toward us. Émise tried again to speak with the old one. One of the young men said, "You must talk to me. I am the only one who understands your language. Who are you and what are you doing here?" Émise said, "We lost our trail. We are here only by accident." The young Taino said, "No one comes here. This is Taino country. It belongs to us. Whoever comes here is an enemy and we have to kill him. No one wishes us good things. The strangers who came in large boats took all our land and made us into slaves." Émise answered, "We did not know it. We did not know anyone was living here. We lost our way. We only want to pass over the ridge. We have been walking all night. When daylight came the trail vanished. The only thing we wanted was food and water. The further we traveled the more lost we became. At last we lay down to sleep, not knowing which way to go."

The man translated for the others. They all laughed and brought their spears down. The old man turned his head and whistled. A small brown dog with white spots came trotting out of the brush and sat next to him. Then the old man motioned for us to come with him, which we did, and the others fell in line behind us. They were all laughing and talking, but we could not understand what they were saying. Jean-Jacques whispered to Émise, "Is it for good or bad?" Émise answered, "I don't know. We will have to wait and see." In time we came to a cluster of five houses, a kind of lacour. But I had never seen houses like these. Though they had thatched roofs, they were round instead of square, and there was no lime on the wattled walls. Each of them had a colored banner at its pointed top. They were close together in a semicircle facing a small courtyard where women were grinding grain on flat stones. More men and boys appeared. There was excited conversation. Our captors seemed to be explaining how we were found. At a certain moment everyone burst into laughter. Émise asked the young man who spoke Creole what they were laughing about. He told us in good humor, "We are laughing because you said the trail disappeared under your feet. We never heard of a trail disappearing. A trail is always there. You meant to say that you disappeared from the trail."

The old man sat on a mat in the courtyard, and his dog came and lay down nearby. Other mats were put down for us, and we sat facing him. A young girl brought him a carved wooden breastplate, which he hung on his chest, and a highly polished black stone which he tied around his wrist. Then we were brought gourds containing a whitish liquid. He motioned for us to drink, which we did. It was not ordinary water but it quenched our thirst. The young girl replenished our gourds and we drank again.

The old man began to speak, and the young translator repeated his words in Creole. He said, "I am Coana, cacique of all the Taino people. We have many villages on the mountain, over there, over there, over there in all directions. This is our country. Once our people covered all this land, right down to the sea. We grew our food and took fish from the ocean. The pale people came. They tried to make us slaves. We resisted. They killed us with muskets, they drove us with whips. Many of our people escaped in canoes, many died working in the fields. But some of our grandfathers said, 'No, we refuse to die or run away. We will go up above in the mountains, where they will leave us alone.' We came up here. Here we live. No pale people come here. No dark people come here. We are living in peace. Only one thing is missing for us. We do not have much fish. We have ponds with small fish in them, but it is not enough. Did you bring any fish with you?" All the Tainos laughed at the joke.

Coana said, "We do not know who you are. We do not know if you are peaceful or evil. We cannot have any evil people in our country. If you are evil we will kill you. Though you might be peaceful we cannot keep you here and you will have to go away—even if the trail disappears from under your feet." Again everyone laughed, though we did not think the joke was amusing. Coana went on, saying, "Now you will have to tell us your story and why you are here, and when you are finished we will decide what to do."

The people of the village crowded around in a circle. They brought a carved wooden staff for Coana to hold in his hand. He replaced his woven cap with a headdress made of parrot feathers. Through his interpreter Coana said, "Explain to us how you came to be here."

Émise said, "Have you people never seen what is down below in the valley? Surely you have seen it many times from the edge of the ridge." Coana said, "We have seen it. Our scouts have brought us reports. It is a place of devils. We know you came from the valley, therefore you must be devils." Émise replied, "You speak well. It is a place where devils rule, but most of the humans down there are merely unfortunate people who have been turned into helpless slaves. They are almost dead and cannot do anything to help themselves. The spirits that gave them life have been removed from their bodies. The devils say this and that, and the slaves must do whatever the masters say. They cannot even talk to one another. But once in a while a slave regains consciousness. Life comes into his head again. Then he tries to escape. Because I accidentally drank salt water my head became clear. I knew that if we tried to go across the other ridge they would catch us with the aid of their grey pigs. Therefore in the black of night my two friends and I escaped from the valley on this side." He told his story, though leaving out numerous details that the Tainos would not understand. The chief picked up a feathered wand and held it in front of Émise. The feathers became agitated and bent over to touch Émise's chest right above his heart. The chief said, "The feathers say your story is true." He then called on Jean-Jacques to speak. Jean-Jacques told his story, beginning with his departure from home. And when he was finished, the chief tested him with the feathered wand. He said, "The feathers say your story is true." When I was told to speak I began with my departure from home, though I left out many things that had happened to me. The chief tested me with his feathered wand, and the feathers bent to touch me where my heart was beating. He said, "Your story is true." Our stories took a long time because they had to be translated, and it was nearly nightfall.

The chief ordered the women and girls to bring us gourds of food, and while we were eating he said, "Now I, Coana, chief of the mountain Tainos, will tell you something. We know all about the devils in the valley. Once they came up here to find more slaves. We did not shout at them to drive them away. We did not wave our weapons. We encouraged them. And when they nearly reached the top we speared them to death and threw their bodies from a cliff. This is the country of the Tainos. The devils will never come again. Sometimes, if we want, we go down and capture corn from their fields, and sometimes when we need meat we kill one of their grey pigs."

A fire was made in the center of the court. A drummer began to play and the women and girls danced a circle dance. We
were offered more of the whitish liquid to drink. One of the
men was a star watcher. When a certain star appeared overhead
he announced it and the festivities came to an end. Jean-
Jacques, Émise and I were taken to a small hut outside the village to sleep. I dropped onto the nearest mat and instantly fell
into a sleep without dreams.

XIV

I was the first to awaken. The sun was already halfway up in the sky. I remained lazily where I was, looking up into the branches of the pines and remembering the events of the previous night. Only slowly did I realize that I should not be seeing the sunlight and the pines, since we had been sleeping in a thatched hut. There were no sounds of voices from the Taino village. Everything was quiet except for birds and tree lizards. I was confused, then alarmed. I got up and looked around me. There was no thatched hut. Nor was I standing on a woven mat but only on loose pine needles.

I went cautiously toward the center of the Taino village. There were no houses there, no sign of any people. Where our divining tests and the women's dance had taken place there was nothing but wild brush. I looked for the remains of our fire but could not find any. There was nothing to suggest there had been a village there at all. I continued exploring and finally said aloud, "It was a dream! There is nothing here."

I returned to the place where we had been sleeping. Jean-Jacques and Émise were sitting up and looking here and there. I said, "I have been exploring. I had a vivid dream that we spent the night in a village, a Taino village." Jean-Jacques answered, "Yes, we did. They fed us and the women gave us a hospitality dance." I said, "Then we both had the same dream." Émise said, "No, I don't believe it was a dream at all. It really happened." I said, "There are no people and no houses. There is nothing, only nothing." The three of us went together. Jean-Jacques and Émise saw what I had seen, only wild brush. They were astonished. Jean-Jacques said, "Here is where we sat. The fire was there in a ring of stones. The chief's mat was facing ours. The women's dance. . . ." He could not say anything more. Émise looked in all directions. For a while he was perturbed and silent. Then he said, "We did not dream it. We all remember everything the same. I have heard of such things. They were ghosts who came from the Taino underworld." I persisted, saying, "No, some spirit gave us all the same dream." Émise shook his head. "Such a thing has never occurred. A dream is given to a person by one of his own ancestors or a vodoun or a baka. We could never have dreamed the same thing."

I asked, "What about the food they gave us? Was it ghost food? And the thatched round houses, were they also ghosts?" Émise said, "Everything has a ghost—trees, rocks, hoes, houses—everything. The whole village was a ghost. I don't understand about the Taino world. It has its own spirits. I believe the village was sent here to help us. Haitian bocors made slaves of us. The whites made slaves of the Tainos. Perhaps the Taino spirits took pity on us." I said, "Possibly they will come back." Émise shook his head. "No, I believe they intended for us to continue on our way. Perhaps in the old days there was a real village on this spot. Maybe the ghosts we saw belonged to the last Taino people who lived here."

At that moment there was a rustle in the leaves and Chief Coana's little brown and white dog came trotting out of the underbrush. He lay on the ground in front of us and wagged his tail. Jean-Jacques said, "But the chief's dog, is he a ghost or not? He is a real dog, as you can see." We did not know what to think. We patted the dog, which acted very friendly. Émise sat down on a large rock and said, "I believe I understand it now.

The village and people were Taino ghosts. The houses were ghosts. Everything that happened was ghostly. The dog also is a ghost, but the chief must have left him behind to help us in some way. Perhaps the dog will hunt for us. Perhaps he will lead us somewhere. We will see."

We set off in a direction we believed would take us across the ridge. The dog went to the front and occasionally turned his head to see if we were following. It was as if he were the leader of a carnival procession. But at one place he turned abruptly to the right and stopped to make sure we were following. Jean-Jacques said, "I don't think that is our direction." Émise said, "I have been watching him closely. He knows what he is doing. We will follow him." We followed the dog. We began to see a faint path. We came to a large rock and saw pictures on it. The rock was so weathered the pictures were not clear. We went on. At a certain place the dog stopped and when we caught up with him we saw we had arrived at a spring. We drank. Émise said, "I was right. The ghost dog is our guide."

Later the dog stopped at some wild berry bushes. Émise said, "The berries are for us to eat." I said, "I have never seen berries like these. They may be poisonous." Émise said he had confidence, and he ate, so Jean-Jacques and I did the same. When the dog went on, we followed. We walked all day, and by early evening we arrived at the far side of the ridge. Ahead in the distance was another ridge. Émise quoted a saying: "Beyond mountains are mountains." The dog changed directions and led us to a cave. On the walls inside were pictures like those we had seen on the large rock. One of the pictures was a human hand. Another was a man holding a spear. We gathered leaves and put them down on the cave floor for sleeping. The dog lay down at the cave opening. We slept.

When we awoke, there was a freshly caught rabbit in front of the cave. But our brown and white dog was not there. We thought he was still hunting, but he did not come back. We skinned the rabbit and ate the meat raw. We lingered until mid-morning, but the dog did not return. At last Émise said, "It is no use waiting, he has gone back to his Taino chief." I had grown very fond of the dog and did not believe Émise. I in-

sisted on waiting a while longer. Finally Émise went to the front
of the cave and said, "Look on the ground. What do you see?"
I looked carefully and answered. "I see our footprints in the
dust." He said, "Yes, and where are the pawprints of the dog?" I
searched. I could not find a single pawprint. I said, "Yes, now
I know you are right. He was a Taino ghost dog." Jean-Jacques
said, "I doubted it, but now I agree." Once more we were on
our own. Before we departed, though, Jean-Jacques made another picture on the cave wall, scratching the rock with the
point of his cane knife. He drew three men and a dog, saying,
"If they ever return they will see this picture." Then we left,
making our way down the farther side of the mountain.

Except for the food we had been given in the Taino ghost
village, I had not had any cooked meat for a long while. I asked
Émise whether he thought we could find fire somewhere. He
said, "Perhaps we will find a village. We can borrow fire there."
I said, "I don't think there are any villages. I have been looking
for smoke everywhere. Where we are going is nothing but wilderness." He said, "If we can find some flint, perhaps we can
strike a fire." We looked for flint as we walked, but we could
hardly see the ground because of the long grass and the deep
pine needles. Émise said, "Do not worry, there are many ways
to bring forth fire. It is everywhere. It is in stones, in wood, and
in the sky." Jean-Jacques said, "Perhaps Hevioso will send
down a thunder stone to light the grass for us." Émise answered, "Yes, it could be. But there is an old saying, 'Don't ex-
pect Hevioso to light your pipe for you.' When we need fire
badly enough we will make it."

We traveled a long while down the steep mountainside,
remembering that when we reached the bottom we would have
to begin another ascent. I began to wonder whether we would
ever find our way out of the mountains, and if we did, where
we would be. I asked Émise if he had some destination in mind,
but he said our purpose for the moment was to get as far from
Habitation Perdue as possible. But we had not seen any trails
and I realized that this wild country was uninhabited, the do-
main of the stern vodoun Maît' Grand Bois, Master of the Great

Forest. I became increasingly anxious. By late afternoon we were nearly at the bottom.

We had not found any flint to spark the fire we needed to cook the remains of our rabbit. Émise said we could try to draw fire out of wood, as he remembered his father doing. What he required was a good hardwood stick and a dry, half-rotted tree branch. Jean-Jacques and I were told to find some dry leaves and rub them into a fine powder with our hands. This we did, and after a while Émise found the stick and branch he needed. He cut a fine point on the stick, placed it against the branch, and began twirling it between the palms of his hands. Sometimes, Jean-Jacques or I relieved him. For a long time nothing happened, and then a fine wisp of smoke became visible. Émise placed some of the powdered leaves around the stick and blew his breath on them gently. Suddenly there was a tiny flame and the powdered leaves began to burn. We added small twigs, then larger ones, and at last we had a fire going. I had never seen anything like that before. We made our camp at that spot and cooked the remains of our rabbit, but we were still hungry. A chilling fog drifted in between the ridges and soon blotted the trees from our sight. We quickly gathered broken branches to keep our fire burning as long as possible, and huddled as close to the embers as we could. The fog muted the usual night sounds, and even though the ground was uncomfortable we lay down and tried to sleep.

Jean-Jacques had not spoken much about how it had been to be a zombie, and if I asked him anything about it he usually said, "I don't remember." But I knew he was having frightening dreams at night because he moaned and jerked his arms and legs and hardly ever lay still. Sometimes he talked in his sleep, but I could not make out the words very well. Often he seemed to be saying, "No, no!" I could only imagine what kinds of things were going through his mind after his experience at Habitation Perdue. I had heard it said that people who recovered from being zombies had nightmares the rest of their lives. Kuku Cabrit once told me there were ceremonies to help cure a person like that, but the ceremonies had to be repeated frequently.

I was too cold to sleep. I put some dry twigs and brush on the fire and when the flames shot up I saw Jean-Jacques thrashing around as if he were in terrible pain. He was breathing very hard and trying to talk, but all I heard were strange sounds in his throat. Once I had heard my mother say that if you awaken someone from an evil dream you should do it very gently in order to leave the evil behind. This I did with Jean-Jacques, shaking his arm gently and saying softly, "My brother, leave it all there and come out here where the fire is. It will make you warm." Soon he opened his eyes, but for a moment he had that empty expression I had seen among the zombie slaves. He asked, as if he was not sure, "Is that you, Dosu?" I said, "Yes, my brother, this is Dosu here. Whatever you saw when you were sleeping, now you have left it behind in that other place."

He sat up and moved closer to the fire. Émise had awakened and was watching Jean-Jacques, but he did not say anything. I asked my brother if his dream had been about Habitation Perdue. He said, "No, not about the Habitation. It was not really a dream. I was there. I was walking in a large courtyard where children were playing." I said, "Ah, can children be anything to worry about?" He said, "These children were different. They were very old." I said, "But children cannot be very old." He answered, "Yes, young like children but old, older than our grandfather Djalan was when he died. They were abiku, the ones that die young and keep being born over and over again. Some of them seemed familiar as though I had seen them somewhere before. They called my name and asked me to play."

I said, "Jean-Jacques, that should not be frightening." He said, "One of them grasped my hand. He said, 'I will take this one, Jean-Jacques from the Red Mountains.' I cannot tell you what he meant. There was an argument among the children. They all claimed me. I wanted to run but there was no place to go. Then you wakened me." I tried to soothe him, saying "You were dreaming that way only because you were cold and hungry." He said, "No, it was not a dream. The abiku boy wanted to keep me there in that place." Émise nodded. Yes, I believe you were in the land of the abiku. But perhaps the boy only thought that if anything should happen to you he could take your place. Or perhaps he wanted to be your next child." Jean-Jacques asked, "Could he cause me to die?" Émise said, "No, I never heard anyone say that an abiku could cause anyone to die. Do not think any more about it. You have merely been to a place others have never seen, that is all." But neither my brother nor I could sleep any more that night, and we spent our time tending the fire.

When we started out in the morning Jean-Jacques was very depressed. I myself became anxious about not knowing where we were going, and at last I told Émise that I was sure the direction we were traveling was not the direction of my home, but just the opposite. He said, "Well, you can go anywhere you want. I am going to the crest of the next ridge. From there we ought to be able to see where we should go. If you want to part here, it is all the same to me." I began to recollect all the good things Émise had done for us and felt ashamed. I also began to wonder who he was and where he came from. He seemed to have more connaissance than most habitants. I said, "Yes, Émise, forgive me. You have been very kind to help us, even when you yourself were being pursued. If we have the strength, we will go to the next ridge with you. Thank you for helping us." He answered, "You will have the strength. I am certain that before too long we will find something to eat."

Eventually we came to the narrow floor of the valley. We found a stream running through it, and this was a good sign because there would be some kind of game nearby. The water refreshed us a great deal. Émise walked upstream examining the ground for signs of game. Suddenly Jean-Jacques groaned. He was looking the opposite way, downstream, at a young boy standing in the water watching us. Then the boy moved away and disappeared into the brush. I said to my brother, "There are people here!" Jean-Jacques kept staring at where the boy had been standing. He said, "He is the abiku who grasped my hand and said, 'I will take this one.' I said, "My brother, do not be agitated. It was only an ordinary boy. His people must live nearby." Jean-Jacques said, "No, Dosu, I recognized him."

I called Émise back and told him what we had seen and

what my brother had said. He shook his head. "I have never heard of such a thing. An abiku cannot reappear among the living until he is reborn. Still, let us see if something is there." I followed Émise downstream, Jean-Jacques lagging behind. Where we had seen the boy there was a pool, and above it a trail wended into the bush. Émise said, "You see, there are people here and they come to the pool for water. Possibly they can give us something to eat." My brother followed Émise and me but he was not reassured. Not far off, the trail opened into a clearing with a thatched house and a garden.

An old man was squatting in the doorway sharpening his sickle with a stone. We greeted him and in reply he nodded his head without speaking. We explained that we had come over the mountain and had had very little to eat. He turned toward the house and struck the sickle several times with the stone. An old woman came out and he asked her to find a little food for us. She brought a calabash bowl of cooked plantains and black beans, which she placed on the ground in front of us. When we were through eating, the old man put his sickle away and said, "The affairs of the sheep are not the affairs of the goat, so I don't ask questions. As for me, I am Tonton Mulet and my wife's name is Lydia. My father was a marron. He came up here to escape the French. He built his house here, where I live to this day. My children and grandchildren have their own habitations up the mountainside."

We announced our names to the old man and his wife, but did not say very much about ourselves. He said, "A name does not say much about a person's life, but already I know something about you. Since I have been living here, very few strangers have come across that mountain. All of them were from That Certain Place on the other side. No doubt so are you. One of them had to be assisted every step by his companion. He could not speak and did not seem to understand anything. His body and his head-spirit had not yet come back together. I made a special lotion for him and he began to recover. One had been maimed by the grey pigs and had a wooden leg. Two were naked and I gave them clothes. In time they all moved on, east or west."

Émise told the old man how we escaped from Habitation Perdue. Tonton Mulet listened quietly, whittling a stick with his sickle and nodding his head. When he finished, I asked, "Grandfather, you spoke of making a special lotion. Is that your profession? Are you a gangan?" He said, "I have knowledge of certain things." He looked at the markings on Émise's legs, the small crosses, and said to him, "I see the insignia on your legs. Do you know what they mean?" Émise said, "They were given to me when I was very young. They are the marks of my father's secret fraternity. He is no longer alive, but he always told us he belonged to the Efik nation. Sometimes the fraternity met in a secret place outside the town of Aquin."

Tonton Mulet asked, "Did he ever mention the word Egbo?" Émise answered, "Yes, yes, Egbo was the name of his society. Now I remember." The old man stood up abruptly and clapped his hands. He said, "Ah! Ah! Those marks tell me you were pledged by your father to the fraternity. They were to be your passport, wherever you went. You are my blood nephew. Stand up, follow me." He motioned for me and Jean-Jacques to come with them. We entered the house, and when our eyes became accustomed to the dim light we saw that the largest wall was hung with flags, bundles of feathers, beaded rattles, and a forged iron bell. In the corner of the room were two ancient, half-decayed drums, and in center of the main wall was a painted design of four small crosses like those on Émise's legs. Tonton Mulet said, "There it is! Egbo!" After that he took us outside again and asked his wife to prepare more food.

I said, "Grandfather, it is the first time I ever saw Egbo. We do not have it in my part of the country." He said, "No, it is nowhere else. I am the last of the brotherhood. All the others are gone. Your friend Émise came close, but he was never initiated. Yet his father was my blood brother. I am an anasaco. When Egbo was still here in Haiti, when I had numerous blood brothers, I used to divine, heal, and prepare attack magic for the fraternity. In Calabar, where we came from, we were numerous and powerful. Without our permission no one could make a journey, or sell trade goods, or forge iron. Even great chiefs came to ask our permission for this and that. But in Haiti it is nearly finished. I am the last part, and when I die, my house will be burned down, leaving nothing behind."

I asked the old man if the Egbo had vodouns. He said, "About things like that, every member made up his own mind. What we all shared together was Leopard, the spirit of Leopard. From him we drew our strength. Perhaps it is because we do not have Leopard in Haiti that we have disappeared." He looked at Émise's legs. "Yet who can tell? If my blood nephew can appear over the mountain like this, perhaps, somewhere, there are still others."

When it was time to sleep, Tonton Mulet took us to a small lean-to behind his house. We lay down, but Jean-Jacques could not sleep. He woke me up, saying, "Dosu, you see now what I was telling you. Only the old man and his wife live here. The boy we saw at the stream does not stay in this house. Now you will believe me when I say he was the same one, the Born to Die, who claimed me in the place of the abiku." I tried to calm him, saying, "But he was far away, we could not really see his features. Perhaps he was just a stray person who came to drink." He said, "No, Dosu, do not play with me like that." I said, "Sleep, now, my brother. In the morning we will ask Tonton Mulet about it."

When we arose at daylight the old lady gave us sweetened coffee for breakfast. Once again Tonton Mulet began sharpening his sickle. At last I said, "Grandfather, are any of your grandchildren living with you?" He said, "No, as I told you, they all live up above." I said, "There is a mystery, and since you are an anasaco possibly you can explain it." He fixed his eyes on mine, waiting. I told him of Jean-Jacques' fearsome dream. Émise said, "But it was not a dream. Jean-Jacques' spirit left his body and went on an expedition to the village of the abiku. Just before we found your path we saw the boy again, standing at the stream."

Tonton Mulet's face became very serious. "There are no children around here." Jean-Jacques said, "Yes, grandfather, we know. That is why I believe the abiku is pursuing me. If he kills me he can be born again to fill my place." The old man took us into his house and sat us down. He took a divining tray from its wrapping of leaves and dusted it off with his hands. He placed it in the center of the floor and emptied a small sack of black beans next to it. Then, in a low voice, he sang some words we could not understand. He said, "These beans were brought here from Calabar. Each bean has in it the spirit of Leopard." He turned to Émise, saying, "Only because you are my blood nephew, through your father, will I perform this divination." Émise said, "Grandfather, we owe you a debt." The old man said, "We don't know if Leopard will respond. He may have more important things to do on the other side of the water." We said, "Yes, we understand." He said to Émise, "Stretch your legs out on both sides of the divining tray, so that Leopard may see the marks." Émise did so.

Tonton Mulet began to recite, again in the language we did not understand, and after a while he threw some of the black beans on the tray and examined them. He closed his eyes and pondered, then cleared the tray and threw again. He continued to recite and call upon Leopard. Then he put the black beans away and said to Jean-Jacques, "Leopard confirmed that you went on the expedition. The abiku child took your hand because he liked you. But he did not behave normally. He was an abiku errant. Somehow he followed you from the abiku place. It was he you saw at the stream, but now he has returned to his home. He thought that if anything happened to you he could be born again and replace you, perhaps with your own name, perhaps some other name. When he saw you at the stream he did not want anything to happen to you. He decided to await his time. But had you fallen on the mountain and killed yourself he would have taken advantage of it. This is what Leopard tells us. Now you may leave something for Leopard, a token of some kind."

Jean-Jacques said, "Grandfather, I would do it gladly, but I have nothing worthwhile to offer." Tonton Mulet nodded his head. I wondered whether I myself had something to give for my brother. All I could think of was my thunder stone, but I was reluctant to part with it. Tonton Mulet reflected on the problem. He said, "A person cannot give more than he has. But you do have something worthwhile, the skin that encases your body and all its inner parts. If you offer a small portion of your skin, Leopard will accept it with understanding." Jean-Jacques answered, "Yes, I will give some of my skin." Tonton Mulet took a sharp knife from the thatch of his house and skillfully cut a small piece of skin from my brother's thigh and placed it in an earthen bowl, saying, "Now it is done."

Then he turned to Émise. He said, "My nephew, I would like to be able to do what you want, but I cannot do it." Émise said, "Grandfather, I have not asked for anything." The old man said, "No you have not asked, but your navel speaks and my navel hears. My blood hears your blood. Your thoughts are about Habitation Perdue and its evil master, Gros Ventre. You would like to repay Gros Ventre for all the evil he has done. Perhaps some great force could do it, but I do not control such a force. Gros Ventre is not a person, he is a unique and powerful baka. There are no others like him. He is indestructible. He has been there since the days of the French. No one knows where he came from. During the Revolution French soldiers passed this way and burned down the Habitation, its buildings and all its crops. The next day everything was back the way it was before. The sugar mill was running again, the master's house was standing, the cane was growing upright in the fields, and the zombie slaves were doing their work. Seven years later the Habitation disappeared completely, and the valley looked as if no humans had ever been there. It was said that Gros Ventre had transported everything to Martinique. But then after seven more years the Habitation suddenly reappeared exactly where it is today. Most vodouns avoid the valley. They would not come there even for a service in their honor. Only Gèdé, Master of the Graveyard, comes to the valley, because he and Gros Ventre are friends. Gros Ventre serves him, though there are those who say Gros Ventre is more powerful than Gèdé himself. Some people have a saying: 'What belongs to the vodouns is theirs, what belongs to Gros Ventre is his.' Go home, live your life, and forget Habitation Perdue."

XV

Later that day Tonton Mulet gave us instructions about how to continue our journey. He told us to go west following the stream. In one day's travel we would emerge from between the ridges and we would find trails going north and south. Émise would turn south toward Aquin, and Jean-Jacques and I would go north toward Anse-à-Veau. In the morning Tonton Mulet's wife gave us each a small knapsack of food, and also a water gourd in case we would need it later. Tonton Mulet gave us a flint for sparking fire. They seemed sorry to see us go. I don't think they saw many people in that place. As we descended the trail to the stream, Tonton Mulet came out of the house with a beribboned hoop in one hand, which he held high in the air, and a cross-shaped rattle which he shook in time to a kind of chant.

We went west along the stream as Tonton Mulet had instructed us, and by evening emerged from between the ridges and found the trails going north to Anse-à-Veau and south to Aquin. We camped for the night, and in the morning when my brother and I were getting ready to continue our way, we saw that Émise was not doing the same. He continued to sit on the ground, sharpening his cane knife, and he looked very troubled. He said, "Do not wait for me. I have one more thing to do. I am going back to the Habitation." We could not believe it. He said, "I have thought of something that can be done to punish Gros Ventre, even if he is a baka. You have seen the govies, those clay jugs sitting on the altars of the Gèdé shrines. Every one of them contains the head-spirit taken from a person when he was changed into a zombie. The spirit is imprisoned there. If it were freed it could go back into the head of the man or woman from whom it was taken. If the head-spirit rejoins its zombie, the zombie will become normal again."

I said, "Yes, I have heard of it, but I do not really understand such things." Émise said, "At a certain hidden place on the Habitation there is a stone warehouse in which hundreds of these govies are stored. Perhaps it is true that a houngan or a bocor or an anasaco may not be able to do anything against Gros Ventre, but an ordinary person like myself can do something. I will get into the warehouse and break the govies. All the head-spirits will be liberated. Where they will go or what they will do I cannot say. Some may go to Yzolé Below the Water, or to Guinée. Some may return to the heads from which they came. Some might even become errant spirits that will wander about and harass the zombie masters. Once they are freed, the head spirits can never again be captured or controlled."

My brother and I could not believe Émise's audacity. We argued, saying, "You yourself are now free. Tonton Mulet counseled you to go home and forget the Habitation." He said, "Tonton Mulet is a good and wise man. But did he ever have to shuffle under a cracking whip from morning till night, hoeing, digging, carrying rocks, cutting cane? Was he made to sing, 'I am only earth?' Did he have a family and friends far away who suffered because of his absence? Did he have his best friends sniffed out or eaten by grey pigs? If his sons were captured by bocors and transformed into zombies would he go home and forget all about it?" We reminded Émise that Gros Venture was not a person but a powerful baka who had an alliance with

Gèdé. He said that no matter what Gros Ventre was, he had made up his mind.

We owed Émise our lives. We did not want to see him go back and perish. But we could not influence him. He got up to leave. Impulsively I took my Hevioso stone from my pocket and gave it to him. He nodded his head and thanked me, saying, "I will use the thunder stone to shatter the govies." He left us, taking a route around the edge of the ridge instead of the trail toward Aquin. When he was out of sight we followed our own trail that went toward Anse-à-Veau. After two days of traveling we began to see houses on the mountainside, and occasionally we met people on the trail. We often looked back toward the direction of the Habitation, which seemed more and more remote in our minds.

On the fourth day after our parting from Émise a dark cloud appeared behind us in the far distance, beyond the ridges we had crossed. My brother said, "The storm looks as if it is above the valley of the Habitation." The cloud grew rapidly until the entire area of the highest peaks was as dark as night. Lightning bolts streaked through the blackness and there was heavy thunder. We felt wind bursting from the center of the storm. Tall trees around us bent like grass, and some of the tallest pines snapped and shattered. We were pelted by tree branches, pebbles and dust, and after that came heavy stinging rain. There was no place to take shelter and we huddled in misery among the rocks. It was as if the sky had broken apart. Suddenly it was all over. The sun shone warmly and we continued our way. That evening we found a grassy place near the trail where we could sleep. We tried to spark a fire with Tonton Mulet's flint, but the leaves and moss were too damp. Fortunately a habitant carrying a pot of difé came along, and we asked if we could borrow from his fire. He came and sat with us until our own fire was burning. He reminded me of my father, and I became very depressed when I remembered that my father would not be home when Jean-Jacques and I arrived there.

The habitant was curious about us, asking where we were going and where we were coming from. I said we were going to the Red Mountains, but was evasive about where we were coming from. He examined us from head to toe for clues, and I believe that somehow he concluded the truth. He picked up his pot of difé, and as he left he said, "Stay on your guard, those people back there have long arms. Also, there are some restless bakas in these hills after dark."

The man's comments had made me uneasy, and there was something about the storm earlier in the day that seemed unnatural, so when I fell asleep I didn't have comfortable dreams. The most vivid dream I had was that when I arrived home there was no one there. Our house had no walls, and the nearest garden had nothing in it but weeds. I wandered around looking for my mother. I started down the trail toward Kuku Cabrit's place and when I went around a certain bend, there, standing in front of me, was Émise Dubois. At first I saw him completely, from head to foot, but somehow his face became enlarged as if we were very close together. He looked into my eyes silently without speaking for a while, then he said, "Dosu, there is no need to worry any more." I asked, "Émise, did you reach Habitation Perdue safely?" He said, "I reached it. I eluded the grey pigs. I broke into the stone warehouse. There were many tables and benches, all of them full of govies with stoppers in their tops, all covered with dust. Every govi had a head-spirit in it, each one from a person who had been made into a zombie. I spoke to the spirits in the govies, saying, 'Be prepared, all you maît' têtes, I, Émise Dubois, am here to release you from your prisons. Go wherever you want, whether to Guinée, to Yzolé Below the Water, or into the head of a newborn person. Do what you please. Torment Gros Ventre if you can, destroy the Habitation if you can, and have pity on all those helpless people who are still zombies. Let them regain their strength and find their way home, or if they are too old and weak, let them die in peace. Be prepared. I am coming.'

"I used your thunder stone, Dosu. I struck a govi and shattered it, then another and another, going from table to table. As each govi broke, something invisible emerged and rushed through the air like wind. Soon it was as if a windstorm was loose in the building, and I was buffeted from every direction. What I was doing became more and more difficult, but I did not stop until every govi was shattered. The roof blew from the warehouse and the stone walls crumbled. A circular wind went up with a roaring sound, sucking up everything with it. It became dark. There were bolts of lightning and loud thunder, and after that an enormous rain with hailstones." I asked anxiously, "And you, Émise, where are you now?" Émise looked very sad. His face began to fade from in front of me. I shouted, "Émise! Émise! Do not go!" But Émise disappeared.

Almost immediately after Émise faded away I found myself talking to Tonton Mulet. I said, "Where is he? What happened to Émise?" Tonton Mulet was sharpening his sickle. He said, "He is there, somewhere, who knows? The spirit of his head went out to join all those who came from the govies. Although I could not do anything to help him, I was there and observed it all." Then Tonton Mulet also disappeared and I awoke. I was lying close to the fire, shivering, though I do not think it was from the cold. When Jean-Jacques awoke I told him of my dream. He said, "You see, Dosu, I was right about the storm."

As we traveled that day we encountered more and more people. We could not yet see the ocean but the air began to smell different. Though sometimes we found ourselves climbing again we had the definite sensation that we were approaching the shore. We came to a place where the trail forked, and we stopped there, not knowing which way to go. A woman coming up from below with a heavy basket on her head also stopped at the fork and we asked her which of the trails would bring us to Anse-à-Veau. She did not answer immediately, but asked us to lower the basket from her head, which we did. She sat down and studied us for a few moments. Then she said, "To the right." We were about to continue our way, but she said, "No, I must rest here for a while. How do you think I can put my basket up again?" So we sat and made conversation with her. When at last she was ready, we lifted the basket and placed it on her head-pad, and after that we resumed our walking. It had rained recently and the red clay was slippery. We had to go carefully, though we wanted to run. We met other habitants along the way, and we were elated that we were well on our way home. When night came we found a grove near the trail where we could sleep. We were happy to see that the trees were of various kinds, even some palms, because that meant we were out of the high mountains where the trees were mostly pines.

We gathered hanging moss from a large tree and Jean-Jacques was trying to spark a fire when a habitant carrying a pot of difé left the trail and came to our grove, saying, "Here, take some of my fire." It was too dark to see him clearly, but when my brother got our own fire going I saw something familiar about the man's face. Suddenly I recognized him—Bocor Zandolite, who had saved me from the fury of the highway vodoun, Legba, divined for me, and given me a passport written by the vodoun Congo Mapiongle. I was astonished to see him again. Even though I had made an engagement with him in exchange for his divination, I had not expected to see him or hear from him until some day far in the future. I said, "Papa Zandolite, forgive me. I did not recognize you in the darkness." He said, "Yes, I know. I see that you have managed to rescue your brother." I said, "Only through the help of Émise, who was a slave at Habitation Perdue." He said, "Yes, the loa Pinga Maza told me when I was divining." I said, "I am afraid Émise is dead. He went back to the Habitation to smash all the govies and never returned." Bocor Zandolite said, "Yes, he died. But Gros Ventre himself was not destroyed. He transported himself to Martinique and took many zombies with him. Some day he will return and the Habitation will come to life again."

I apologized for not having any food to offer him. He opened his straw knapsack and took out some cornbread which he shared with us. Then he said, "Dosu Bordeaux, we have a compact. That is why I am here." I felt very uneasy. I said, "Yes, Papa." He looked into my face seriously, then quoted a familiar saying: "If the drummer comes late he is scolded. When it is time to pay him it is too soon." I said, "Papa Zandolite, whatever it is, I will do it." He said, "The task I have for you must be done immediately." I was discouraged that my brother and I would be delayed. I also feared that Bocor Zandolite would give me something difficult and dangerous to do. Bocor affairs were not like planting maize. He seemed to understand my thoughts. He said, "Our engagement is contained in the earthen jar in the ground. It lives. It will be there until you have paid your pledge. When you have completed your work the jar will break and you will be freed from your obligation." I remembered the penalties for not living up to an engagement. The flesh on my legs would melt away and I would become a dry bone person. And I also remembered the good deeds Bocor Zandolite had done for me. He said, "Let us all sleep now, it is late. In the morning I will tell you what is to be done."

I did not sleep well. I had fearsome dreams. I hoped that when morning came I would find that Bocor Zandolite was also a dream, and that he would not really be there. But when the sun rose he was sitting beside the ashes of the fire. We did not have anything to eat, but Bocor Zandolite gave us some coffee beans to chew. It made us feel better. He said to my brother, "Jean-Jacques, Dosu must do his work alone. You cannot go with him. Continue your journey. It is a long distance, but you will find your way home safely. I will send a message to Kuku Cabrit through his divining board and tell him you are coming." Jean-Jacques was very worried about me, but he said good-bye and left us. I watched him descend the trail until he was no longer visible.

Bocor Zandolite said, "I need you to perform a transference." I said, "Papa, I do not know what a transference is." He answered, "Be patient. Whatever you need to know, I will explain. Though you do not have much understanding of such things, you will be able to accomplish it if you listen carefully and carry out my exact instructions. A transference is exchanging a soul-spirit of a living person for another soul-spirit taken from a person who has died." I said, "Ah, Papa, I am not a houngan or a bocor, I can never accomplish such a thing! Give me some other task to perform!" Bocor Zandolite said, "No, you are not a houngan or bocor, but I can give you the powers you will need. I was assigned the responsibility for this task by the vodoun Pinga Maza. I am indebted to him. He is the guardian of my head, where he often resides. When I call on him for help, he comes. As long as I live we are bound together.

The compact we have is not a spoken one, like yours and mine. But it is there all the same, and when Pinga Maza demands something it must be done.

"An old man I did not know came to me for help, and I began to read the divining board for him. At a certain moment I saw a flash of light and felt something forcing its way into my body from every side. Everything glowed and the old man for whom I was divining changed form. Instead of old he was young and was dressed in a brilliant uniform. Although I had never seen him before, I knew at once who he was. I began singing a song to him:

> *Pinga Maza oh, you are here!*
> *Pinga Maza oh, you are here!*
> *Oh vodoun, I am your horse, ride me!*
> *Oh vodoun, my hounfor is yours, rest here!*
> *Oh vodoun, my children are yours, father them!*
> *Pinga Maza, I thank you for coming!*

"He spoke. He told me of something that had to be done. I was to select a messenger to go to Limbé near Cap Haïtien and perform a transference. There is a man in Limbé named Simon Gros Morne who has done unforgivable things to Pinga Maza. He neglected to hold services for him. When he celebrated the vodouns he failed to call Pinga Maza's name, though he was much indebted to him for many good fortunes in his life. He held no feasts for Pinga Maza. Instead, he adopted other vodouns who he thought could bring him better fortune. When Pinga Maza tried to come to him on the water road, Simon Gros Morne called for Legba to bar his way, causing a battle between the two vodouns which other vodouns joined. Now Pinga Maza has decided to make a transference to replace Simon Gros Morne's soul-spirit, his bon-ange, with one taken from a person now dead."

I asked, "Papa, what will it do to Simon Gros Morne?" He said, "Gros Morne will have the same body, but everything inside of him will change. He will not have the same character. He will behave like someone else. Perhaps he will be someone else, I cannot say." I was dismayed to hear what I was expected to do. I said, "Papa, there must be other tasks you could assign to me instead of this one. I know nothing of the mysteries of the hounfor. I am sure I will never be able to achieve what you are asking." He answered, "Dosu, the empty hole has been filled. What Pinga Maza demands of me I have to do. What I demand, you have to do because of our engagement." I felt more helpless than I had at any time since the beginning of my journey. Bocor Zandolite tried to reassure me, but it did not help. I had a desperate wish that everything going on was a dream, but I knew it was not.

Bocor Zandolite said, "This is what you are to do. Find Simon Gros Morne's house. Enter however you can while he is sleeping. Make Pinga Maza's vèvè design on the floor next to his bed. Hold the govi near his forehead, almost touching. Then say quietly, so as not to awaken him, the words I will give you. Wait until you hear a sound inside the govi. Go out of the house quickly. Now the govi has Gros Morne's bon-ange in it, and the other bon-ange is in Gros Morne's body. Throw the govi on the ground and shatter it. Gros Morne's soul-spirit will depart and go its own way. It will never be heard of again. Perhaps Gros Morne will not wake up, perhaps he will awaken and chase you, who knows? Whatever happens, depart quickly and return here. Your task will be finished."

I said, "Papa, Limbé is a great distance from here, near Cap Haïtien. It will take many weeks to get there and return. When will I ever reach home?" He answered, "How you get there and return is a simple matter. I will help you with that. Now let us work." He began teaching me the words I would have to say, and how to draw the vèvè design with maize meal. First one, then the other, over and over. He said that unless I did everything perfectly, the expedition would fail. I became more and more depressed, certain that I was not capable of doing what he was asking, and greatly troubled that I was being compelled against my will to be an instrument of Bocor Zandolite's magic ceremony. But I could not forget the penalty I would suffer if I refused to keep my engagement. I saw no way to avoid carrying out Bocor Zandolite's demands.

I spent the whole day learning the mystic words, none of which I had ever heard before, and practicing making the vèvè design, though using dry soil instead of maize meal because there was no meal to waste. When Bocor Zandolite believed I had mastered the vèvè design, he tried a cloth around my eyes and instructed me to make the drawing without seeing it, which I found very difficult. He became impatient with me and spoke harshly for the first time. I said, "Papa, I am trying hard. Why must my eyes be covered?" He said, "You will have to do your work at night while Simon is sleeping. It may be very dark and you may not be able to see anything. Therefore you must be able to make your vèvè perfectly even in total darkness." I continued, over and over. In time I began to feel as if I could see through the cloth. Perhaps one of my vodouns was guiding my hand. My drawing became good, then perfect. Finally Bocor Zandolite said I could stop. I took the cloth from my eyes and saw that in fact I had drawn a fine vèvè.

The sun was beginning to set. Bocor Zandolite ordered me to lie on my back, which I did. He took two objects from his knapsack. The first was a small packet of ground maize for making the vèvè. He put it in my hand, saying, "Hold it well." The second was the clay govi containing the soul-spirit of the dead person, which he put in my other hand, saying, "Hold it well." As the sun slid out of sight and the light faded, Bocor Zandolite recited some phrases in Guinée language and placed his hand on my forehead. He sang a little and then recited more Guinée words. My eyes became heavy with sleep. I felt that I was floating up from the ground, and after that all thoughts disappeared from my mind.

XVI

When I awoke it was late afternoon. Bocor Zandolite was not there. I wondered if he had been only one of my disturbing dreams, but I realized that I was holding his govi in one hand and his packet of maize meal in the other. When I was fully awake I saw that I was in a small grove, but it was not the same grove as before. I descended a small trail and reached a road with carriage tracks. When I saw several habitants coming in my direction I quickly wrapped the govi and the packet of maize meal in some long Guinée grass. I asked the men which way I should go to get to Limbé. They laughed and said they were going toward Limbé, on their way home from a coumbite work party, so I walked with them and made conversation. They asked where I came from and I was vague about it, saying, "From the south." They laughed again. They said they knew it from my way of talking. They wanted to know where I was going, and I said I had a message to deliver to Simon Gros Morne from one of his relatives.

One of them said, "Gros Morne? He is a big man around here. He owns a great deal of land. He has one wife at his house and three placée wives at different places."

Another man said, "Oh, he is not so big, it's just that his pants are too tight." They all laughed again, and someone said, "You don't look like a relative of Gros Morne." I hurried to say, "No, no, I am not a relative. I was just employed to bring him a message." He answered, "I am glad of that. He is very rich but he doesn't do anything good for anyone. No one knows how he became so rich. People think he made a compact with a demon of some kind. They say some market women went past his house one time and looked through the door. They saw money falling down from his ceiling and he was busy picking it up and stuffing it into a box." "Just the same," someone said, "he owns everything and we work like donkeys." I asked whether they could tell me where Simon Gros Morne lived. They said he lived in a pink house right where the road entered the town.

I could see Limbé directly ahead, but before reaching it the habitants turned off onto a side trail. Hunger pained my stomach, but I did not have any money. As I passed a woman selling avocados at the roadside I put my hand in my pocket, knowing all the while that there was no money there. I was astonished to find a rag containing several small coins. No doubt Bocor Zandolite had put it there while I was sleeping. So I bought an avocado and after I had eaten it I felt much better.

As I entered Limbé I saw the pink house where the habitants said it would be. I looked at it carefully as I passed, but I did not stop because I did not want to attract any attention. The house had two doors, one in front and one at the side, and there was wooden grillwork all the way around under the eaves. The second story extended out above the front door, and all the windows had white shutters. It was clearly the house of a rich man. All along the street women were sitting in front of their doorways selling bread or fruit. At the far end of the town a blacksmith was forging at the side of his house. Having nowhere else to go I sat down nearby and watched him work. I greeted him politely, but he had no time to answer. Lying on the ground was a long iron bar, one end of it in a fire. At a certain moment, he motioned with his head for me to pick up the cool end, and he set the glowing end on his stone anvil.

After hammering for a while he threw the bar into a long trough filled with water, saying, "Ogoun, merci."

He sat down on a bench and wiped the sweat from his chest and arms with a rag. Finally he looked at me and returned my greeting. He asked me if I was a stranger, where I came from, where I was going, and all the usual questions. I answered most of his questions truthfully, though I said something about going to Cap Haïtien to locate a relative. Then I asked him some innocent questions about the town, and finally commented on the pink house at the other end of the street, saying, "It must belong to a very rich person." He shook his head, saying, "Oh, Gros Morne's place. Sometimes he comes and wants me to make this or that for him. Whatever I make, he's never satisfied with it and complains about the money. His wife is the same way in the market. However, everybody knows he has money buried everywhere. In the ground, under his house, in the walls, in his granary, in his gardens, everywhere. He is a coffee merchant, but no one could make so much money selling coffee. Besides, we don't grow much coffee around here."

He stood up and lifted the iron bar from the water. He held it loosely in his hand to let the water drip away. The bar began to turn gently, rotating until the forged end was pointed toward me. There it stopped. The blacksmith said, "The bar is telling me something. Are you a child of Ogoun?" I said yes, Ogoun was my vodoun, and I showed him the small piece of iron I carried in my clothes. He said, "All blacksmiths have Ogoun in their heads. If not for Ogoun we could not be masters of iron."

He worked again on his anvil. When he stopped, he said, "Ogoun also gives blacksmiths keen perception, so I know you are not going to Cap Haïtien. And I know you have a special mission in Limbé." I did not answer. He said, "Use the side door, it has a feeble bolt inside. Pry it open with your machete." He said nothing more, and after a while I thanked him and left.

I wandered around the countryside at the blacksmith's end of the town for a while, then returned to Simon Gros Morne's end. This time I walked more slowly past the pink house, trying to memorize the outside and imagine what the inside was like, but I learned nothing new. When daylight began to fade I settled down in some heavy brush and waited. Darkness came, but for quite a while the town was still awake. Little by little the lamps went out, and most of the town slept. Dogs barked back and forth in the distance, but I didn't hear any dogs around Gros Morne's place, which surprised me, because I thought a rich person would have three or four watchdogs. Here and there thin fragments of light leaked through Gros Morne's shutters. In time, the oil lamps on the lower floor were extinguished, and light came through the shutters only at one corner of the upper floor, so I decided that was where he slept. When that part of the house became totally dark I assumed Gros Morne had gone to bed.

But I wanted to be sure he was sleeping before I did anything, so I waited. There were stars in the sky, but they were dim. Soon the moon rose and everything became bright. I could see the street and the houses clearly. I became very nervous, thinking I would surely be seen by someone, yet the moonlight would also be helpful to me. At last I knew it was time to go. I unwrapped the govi and the packet of ground maize and approached Simon Gros Morne's house, staying as much as possible in the shadows. I went to the side door, as the blacksmith had told me to do, and used my machete to pry it open. The moonlight filtered through the shutters and I saw stairs directly in front of me. I went upstairs to the corner room where Gros Morne slept. I could see a bed enveloped in a mosquito netting suspended from the ceiling. Vaguely I saw two people in the bed. Both were snoring loudly. Which one was Simon and which one his wife?

I was terrified about carrying out my task. If I were caught what would I do? Finally I crept silently to the bedside and saw that the person closest to me had a beard, so I knew it was Simon Gros Morne. I opened my packet of meal and made Pinga Maza's vèvè on the floor. The moonlight filtering through the shutter made it possible to faintly see what I was doing. The vèvè was not perfect, but it was better than I thought it would be. After that I opened the mosquito netting and placed the govi close to Gros Morne's forehead and whispered the mystic words Bocor Zandolite had taught me. They began with the words 'Pinga Maza Papa,' but the other words were all in ritual language and I didn't understand them. Just as I finished, Simon Gros Morne turned his head and I was afraid I would not get out of the house safely. At that moment I heard a sound like wind inside the govi, which meant I could now leave. At the very same moment Simon's wife woke up and saw me. She screamed, and Simon also woke up. I fled down the stairs as fast as possible. When I was outside I smashed the govi on the ground and ran. I heard Simon Gros Morne trying to arouse the town and looked back. He was standing at the door waving his arms. I did not look back again, but kept running until I was far away in the countryside.

I was breathing heavily and my heart was pounding hard. I had no idea of what my actions had done to Gros Morne, but knew I had performed my task. I resumed walking, anxious to get as far from Limbé as I could. In time I felt exhausted and lay down in some tall grass near the road. I thought I would rest a while and then continue my way. Shortly thereafter, however, I fell into a deep, black sleep.

When the sun woke me up I lay for a while and thought about the events of the night, wondering if I should not get up instantly and try to find out which way to go to get home. But something puzzled me. I was not lying in tall grass near Limbé, but in a small grove of pines, and I realized it was the same grove where Bocor Zandolite had come to my brother and me and offered us fire from his difé. Slowly I recalled everything. I remembered that Bocor Zandolite had sent me to the town of Limbé to carry out a transference on a man named Simon Gros Morne. I did not recall making any journey to Limbé. I had simply found myself there. I remembered carrying the govi and the maize meal. I remembered the blacksmith. I remembered breaking into Gros Morne's pink house, making the vèvè, holding the govi to Gros Morne's head, and breaking the govi as I escaped. I recalled even the smallest things. But how did I get there, and how did I return to the place where I started? Obviously Bocor Zandolite, with his extraordinary mystic powers, had accomplished it. In some way he had transported me to Limbé and brought me back.

Or perhaps it had all been a dream. Maybe Bocor Zandolite had not really come to this place and told me I had to do these things. Yes, probably I had dreamed it. Yet how was it that I remembered the magic words he had taught me, and the vèvè I had to make for Pinga Maza? As I stood up I saw that bits of maize meal clung to my clothing, and that there was more meal on my hands and between my fingers. Now I was certain that everything had really happened. Jean-Jacques was not there with me because Bocor Zandolite had ordered him to go on ahead. I felt very tired, probably from my frantic running to escape from Simon Gros Morne's house, but I continued my way on the Anse-à-Veau trail. Though I was resentful about the ordeal Bocor Zandolite had put me through, I was relieved that my pledge to him was paid and that he was finished with me. Still, I did not forget that he was helpful to me when I needed him.

I reached Anse-à-Veau the next day. When I passed a bread vendor at the roadside I realized that I had not eaten for a long time, but I knew I had no money. I felt through my knapsack and pockets for something I could trade for bread. In one corner of my knapsack I touched something wrapped in a small piece of rag. I took it out and saw with astonishment that it was the little packet of coins Bocor Zandolite had given me for my expedition to Limbé. There wasn't much money in it, but enough to buy a loaf of bread, and I felt very fortunate. But seeing those coins reminded me again of my frightening journey to Limbé, and I hoped nothing like that would ever happen to me again. When Bocor Zandolite had buried my pledge in the ground behind his house, he had told me that once my pledge had been paid the jar would break and I would have no more obligations to perform for him. I hoped it would prove to be so.

Eventually I came to Ville Cochon, the fishing village where I had been brought by Dumé La France's relative, Aubelin Saline. It made me feel better to know that little by little I was getting closer to home. And suddenly I remembered Félicie

Moreau, who had been so kind to me when I was in her village. I had hardly thought of her since then, but now I had a great desire to see her. I hoped she was still there, and became disturbed at the possibility that she might have moved away.

The old route from Ville Cochon to the village where Félicie lived was very bad because it had been washed away by the sea. In addition there had been landslides which had completely blocked the way. I realized how fortunate I had been when Dumé La France persuaded Aubelin Saline to bring me to Ville Cochon in his boat. People had made a new foot trail into the hills to reach one village from the other, but they were so steep and rocky that they were of no use whatever for oxen, or even for donkeys. The trail went across a range of hills into a valley and then toward the east, but there were so many forks and cross trails that it was quite easy to become lost. I had been walking almost half a day when I met two habitants who told me I was going toward a place called Trou Dondon, far out of my way. They said I would have to go back until I reached the sea trail, otherwise I would end up in some nearly uninhabited mountains. So I went back with them until they reached a private path that went to their own house. They gave me a description of the place where I would be able to get on the correct trail—a certain pile of fallen rocks, a certain grove of trees, a broken pine, and so on, for which I thanked them, though I was certain I would never recognize these landmarks when I saw them.

I was right about this, because so many groves looked alike and I never saw the broken pine they described. In the late afternoon, judging from the sun, I concluded that I was going altogether in the wrong direction, but I followed the trail I was on, fearing that if I left it I would become totally lost. I came to an overhanging slab of rock under which I could stay until morning, and I ate some of my bread and fell asleep.

When I awoke, the sun was already up in the sky. I was surprised to see someone sitting on the ground sharing my shelter with me, a ragged old man without any teeth. I greeted him, happy to see another person in this wilderness. He did not say anything, but gave me a toothless grin. It was only then

I noticed the crotch-cane in his lap, and I recognized him as the old man I had met in Dleau Frète when I made Legba's sign in the dust, the one who had spun around on his crotch-cane and then disappeared in the mist. My spirits fell. After all my miseries Legba was still pursuing me. I said, "Respect, Papa of the Highway. Do not make my life harder. I have been on a difficult and painful journey. I only want to go home." He said, "Dosu Bordeaux, I know where you have been and everything you have done. Though you were not aware of it, I helped you many times. Do you think anyone could make such a journey without my assistance?" I said, "Thank you, Papa, for everything you did for me," though I could not remember anything he did except to mount my head that night on the trail and knock me around until I became unconscious.

He said, "Ah, yes, that time I mounted your head and rode you. You cursed me and called for my crotch-cane to be eaten by beetles. I only wanted to give you a taste of what you were dealing with." I said, "Papa, I regret it. I was too sorry for myself, and I didn't understand." He said, "That was one time I saved you. I arranged it so you would be found by Bocor Zandolite. He came and took you home." I said, "Thank you, Papa, I am grateful." He said, "Do not forget that I am a hard vodoun. Ogoun is a hard vodoun, Sobo is hard, Damballa is hard, but I am the hardest of all. I am on every highway and at every crossroad, though people may not see me. If I feel good I keep people on the right road, if I am cross I send them anywhere I want. Sometimes, for a joke, I even send vodouns in the wrong direction so they arrive late where they are going."

I was fearful of what he was going to do to me this time. He did not seem angry. Rather he seemed amused at the tricks he had played on other vodouns. At last he arose and placed his crotch-cane under his withered leg. He said, "Dosu, I am going to keep you on the right trail until you reach home. If you are perplexed, simply say, 'Papa Legba, open the gate for me.'" I said, "Thank you Papa." He went outside the slab shelter and began walking. I also went out. I thought he had descended toward a grove of trees on the edge of a deep gully, but I couldn't see him there. I looked in other directions, but he had totally disappeared, just as he had that time at Dleau Frète.

Somewhere along the trail, after seeing no other people, I stopped and said quietly, "Papa Legba, open the gate for me." It was not exactly a sound I heard. I seemed to feel a voice inside my head. It said, "Continue, continue." Some time later I came to a place where three trails converged, and again I said, "Papa Legba, open the gate for me." Once more I felt the voice in my head. "Take the trail to the right." In time I came to another trail and Legba said, "This one is yours." I was very happy and made up a little song of thanks for Legba:

> *Papa Legba, Legba Papa,*
> *I am your child of the highway,*
> *Thank you Papa Legba*
> *For guiding me in the wilderness.*

I was now on the main trail that twisted and turned but finally came down to the sea.

XVII

It was evening when I reached Félicie
Moreau's village. The fishermen were on the
shore hanging up their nets or unloading
their catches from their boats. I stopped at
the edge of the village, nervous about entering. I could not understand my agitation.
However, when I saw Dumé La France
down among the boats I went to where he
was working. He recognized me and
smiled, saying, "Ah, you have arrived. I did
not know if I would see you again. I didn't
know if the zeaubeaups or the lougaros
might have eaten you." I said no, nothing
had eaten me, as he could see, but it had
been a difficult journey and I was glad to be
going home. He said, "I heard that you
found Habitation Perdue." I wondered how
he could know anything like that. He said,
"No, I am not a bocor or a houngan. Your
brother passed through here a week ago
and asked us to watch for you." I was
happy to hear about Jean-Jacques. "He told
us a few things, not much, only that he had
been on the Habitation and that you had
brought him out. Also that the Habitation
had been destroyed by a man named
Émise." I felt sad to hear Émise's name.
  My eyes were drawn to the higher

ground where women were working in their courtyards. Dumé asked, "Are you looking for any special person?" I said no, I was just refreshing my memory of the village. He said, "That is good. I thought you might be looking for someone in particular. That would be too bad. She went away to live with her mother." My disappointment must have been very obvious. Dumé laughed and said, "No, don't pay any attention. Go and find her. We can talk later. Everyone wants to hear your story."

I went to Félicie's house. She was not there, so I sat on the bench by her door. I fell asleep sitting up, and then after a while I heard her voice saying, "Well, so you have turned up again like a dead fish washed up by the tide." I said, "Yes, I am here." She busied herself with her winnowing tray as if I were not there, made a fire, and set a pot over it, ignoring me as much as she could. After doing a number of things she looked at me as if she were noticing me for the first time, saying, "Ah, I think I remember you. Isn't your name Joseph Lemaire? No, Alphonse Lemaire. There have been so many young men passing through here I cannot recall their names." I said, "Félicie, you know me very well, Dosu Bordeaux." She answered, "Oh, yes, Dosu Bordeaux." She looked at me with concern, saying, "What have you done to yourself? You are very thin. You do not really look so much like Dosu Bordeaux."

She went into the house and came out with a piece of soap. She said, "Go down to the water and wash." I took the soap and went to the shore, where I removed my clothes and bathed. It made me feel better. I ran back and forth on the sand until I was dry, then put my clothes on again and returned to Félicie's house. She was cooking black beans and rice, with bits of clam mixed in. When it was cooked she filled a gourd with it and told me to sit on the bench and eat. I don't remember ever eating anything so good. All the while I was eating I was watching Félicie, trying to judge her feelings.

I said, "I went to that place, Habitation Perdue. I didn't think I would ever find it. Many hard things happened on the way. I encountered vodouns and several kinds of demons. There were too many things to remember in the right order. But I found the Habitation, and because the vodouns were with me,

I found my brother, Jean-Jacques. For his friend, though, I was too late and could not do anything for him. The world back there in the mountains is full of evil things and mysteries. Some of them you cannot see, but they are around you all the time. There are houngans serving the vodouns, and bocors doing magical things. I even met a white bocor in a black robe. And the zombies, I saw many of them at the Habitation. The story is too long for now, but I will tell you little by little as it comes to my mind."

Félicie said, "You are thin. I can see your bones. I will have to put some flesh on your arms and legs. Tomorrow I will wash your clothes so you won't smell so bad." We shared her mat that night, and when I awoke in the morning she was not there. My clothes too were gone. All the small objects which had been in my pockets or tied inside my shirt were piled neatly on the table. An old but clean pair of pants was hanging on a peg, and I put them on. When Félicie came back, my own clothes were already dry but she would not let me have them. She said she was going to repair the holes first. She began right away. I looked through my possessions and when I saw the piece of dog tail that had been fastened inside my shirt I thought of Mama Musoka, who had given it to me to protect me from bizangos. I asked Félicie about her, and she said, "Ah, Mama Musoka will live forever."

While Félicie was sewing I went to Mama Musoka's house on the road to Petit Goâve. I knocked on her door post and waited for an invitation to enter. She called out, "What do you Nagos want now? Always something. It is Mama Musoka this and Mama Musoka that. This is a Moundongue house. Leave me alone. But if you have a conch to keep me alive, bring it in." I said, "Mama, I will bring you a conch later. I just wanted to greet you and let you know I have come back." She squinted at my face and said, "Oh, it is you, the crazy boy who went to Habitation Perdue. Were you bothered by bizangos? I told them to let you alone." I answered, "No, Mama, they did not bother me. I did not see one on the whole journey." She said, "Do you still have the dog's tail?" I said yes, I still had it. She said, "Good, keep it safe. The bizangos will stay away. When you

bring me the conch, also bring a red snapper and some crabs."
I said I would do that, and returned to Félicie who was just
finishing with the sewing.

That night while we were eating I told Félicie I wanted to
take her back to the Red Mountains to stay with me. She said,
"Oh, you think you are too good to stay here and be a fisherman?" I said, "I don't know anything about the sea. I don't have
my own boat, either. But at home I have land, and I know how
to farm. My mother is alone because my father died while I was
away and she needs someone to help her." She said, "Oh, now
I understand. You need me to take care of your garden and
carry your yams to market." I kept telling her how much she
would like it and she kept teasing me without giving me any
sign that she was taking me seriously. Yet I felt very happy
when we were on her sleeping mat at night, and it seemed that
she liked me very much.

The next day was Sunday and most of the men did not go
out to fish, but sat around the boats mending their nets. I went
to see Dumé La France, who was putting pitch on his boat, and
soon he had me talking about my journey and all the experiences I went through. Some of the other men joined us and
listened as if I were Toussaint L'Ouverture himself. When I told
how the spirits from the govies had destroyed Habitation Perdue they wanted to know more and more, and when I told
them how the Habitation had been transported to Martinique
by Gros Ventre, some of them said yes, their fathers or grandfathers had told them that many years ago it had happened the
same way. They were fascinated with the description Émise had
given me when he came to me in my dream and told me how
he had broken the govies with my thunder stone and liberated
the head-spirits. One man said that he knew from his experience as assistant to a certain houngan that when a head-spirit
was liberated from a govi a wind always came out of the shattered vessel, often with a whistling sound. I told them about
my meetings with Bocor Zandolite, and how he had sent me on
the expedition to Limbé to pay off my engagement. They
wanted to know how the transference of Gros Morne's soul-
spirit had changed him, but I could not say anything about that

because I did not know Gros Morne, and also because I had fled so quickly when my work was done. However, it was taken for granted that the transference would seriously affect his fortunes and that he would end up as a poor and worthless person, perhaps a vagabond.

Some of the men began to talk about the difference between a head-spirit and a soul-spirit. One or two said they were the same thing, but Dumé La France became impatient and said, "You are all saying this or that, but you do not know anything. A person's head-spirit is the vodoun who uses your head as a reposoir. When you are mounted, your vodoun comes from Guinée or wherever he may be and enters your head and makes you do whatever he wants. He rides you like a horse, and makes you do things that are his signature. In this way we can see which vodoun has entered. If you act like a soldier at war, that is Ogoun in your head. If you wriggle on the ground like a snake, that is Damballa or Ayida. If you claw with your hands and eat uncooked meat, that is Sebo the leopard.

"But your soul-spirit, that is something else. It does not come, go away and come back, or guard your house like a head-spirit does. It is there when you are born. It looks like you in every way, but it cannot be seen. While you are alive, you are just its covering. If you do something good, it is your soul-spirit, your bon ange, that is really doing it. When you die, your bon ange does not die, it goes to the place of all our ancestors, either in Guinée or below the water. If you hear the voice of your grandfather coming from a spring, that is his bon ange, his soul-spirit, speaking to you. Your bon ange is your character. Without it you are nothing. When Dosu performed the transference Bocor Zandolite instructed him to do, Gros Morne's soul-spirit was extracted from his body and replaced by some other soul-spirit. Gros Morne was no longer Gros Morne. Who he became is not known to us."

One old man nodded his head all the while Dumé was speaking. He said, "Dumé is right. Some houngans say everyone has two soul-spirits, a gros bon ange and a petit bon ange, though I do not know the difference. But I do know this. When I was young there was a man in our village named Saltrou who was not a good person. He fought with everyone. If someone's chicken wandered near his house he took it and had his wife prepare it for dinner. Whenever he made commerce with someone he cheated him in one way or another. He seduced the wife of his own brother. People kept saying, 'How can we live with such a bad man in our village?' Then one time he went too far. He seduced his brother's daughter.

"His brother went to see a strong bocor who lived in a cave and asked what could be done. The bocor divined with shells and told him he could remove that bad person's bon ange and imprison it in a tree. I cannot tell you how it was accomplished, because I was only a young boy then and did not understand such things. But the bocor sent an expedition against Saltrou. It cost a great deal of money. However it was done, Saltrou's bon ange was removed and transferred into a tree. The tree suffered greatly. Its limbs became gnarled and twisted, and people said they sometimes heard it moan. As for Saltrou himself, he no longer had a soul-spirit. He could not speak, he could not understand. He was empty, like a zombie. In time his wife left him and he lived alone until he died. They did not hold a death service for him, simply carried his body somewhere far from the village and left it there."

Someone said, "Ah, I heard of something like that in my village. A certain man's soul-spirit had been taken from his body. When he died, he was buried at the edge of a busy road so that his bon ange could find his grave if it wanted to be reunited. They did the same thing if a person was struck with lightning." Dumé said, "Yes, they did that, but it was not the same. If Hevioso or Sobo struck someone with lightning, that was because the person had offended the vodoun in some way. They did not bury him in the graveyard because that would contaminate all the other dead buried there. Instead, they buried him at a busy roadside so that he would not get any rest. Usually the people did not like to walk so near such a grave, and they would make a new trail so they could go around it."

I had not heard such things before and was impressed with how much I didn't know. It was getting late, and I went back to Félicie's house to ask her again to come away with me. She said,

"No, Dosu, why should I go into the mountains and be a habitant's wife? I like it here. Why should I leave all my friends behind? As for a man, there are plenty of them who want to be fishermen. You could learn. You could work with Dumé until you save enough money to get your own boat." I tried everything I could think of to persuade her. I said I was leaving the next morning, and all she needed to do was to pack her clothes and pots in a saddle basket and I would carry it for her. She said if I stayed and became a fisherman we could live together, otherwise I could go on my own way and be a mountain man. She went to her mortar to grind grain, and while she was pounding she sang:

> *When you lose your mother, you cry.*
> *When you lose your father, you cry.*
> *When you lose a man, what is that to concern you?*
> *Men are everywhere, the world is full of them.*

In the morning when I was preparing to leave, Dumé and some of the other village people came to say goodbye. One woman gave me some fresh baked bread, and Dumé's wife gave me a woven straw knapsack in which to carry my possessions. Félicie gave me a straw sun hat to wear. I felt very fortunate and was reluctant to leave. Dumé told me not to go back to the Red Mountains the same way I had come. He said there were too many mysteries and potent forces at work along that trail. He advised me to go along the main road to Petit Goâve, where I would find many trails that would take me where I was going. "Of course," he said, "you may find bakas up there, but that is the way it is in the mountains. Don't forget to call on Legba often, also Ogoun. The vodouns can be harsh or gentle. They appreciate it if you don't forget them." He took me aside and gave me a polished black stone. "It is a loa stone, a vodoun stone. A vodoun lives in it." He blew on it and it became moist. "You see, the loa sweats. That is how you know it is there and breathes. Take care of it." I thanked Dumé and said I would remember him. I looked at Félicie once more with the faint hope she had changed her mind, but she was gazing over my head out to sea. So I resumed my journey alone, going east toward Petit Goâve.

Before arriving at Petit Goâve, however, I came to a crossroad where market women were selling produce, and I asked them about the best route to Dleau Frète. Hardly anyone had heard of it, but an old man said, "I was there once when I was young. Why would anyone go to so much trouble to get to that place?" I said my family lived in the mountains above Dleau Frète and I wanted to get home by the shortest trail possible. He said yes, I certainly talked like a mountain person. Did I have any goats at home? It was a good place for goats, the land was so rocky. I thought at first that he was ridiculing me, but as he kept talking I realized that he was somewhat simple and said whatever came into his mind. He said that if I followed the cross trail it would take me through the marshy flats that ran along the shore and to the first range of hills. After that the trail would mount the first range, on the other side of which there would be other trails going toward the Red Mountains. He remembered very well that there was an old cemetery near the intersection of the trails, and close to the cemetery was a Gèdé shrine and reposoir. A woman selling plantains interrupted him, saying, "Papa, that was many years ago. Nothing is the same after all those years."

He said, "Oh, you young ones. You have not been anywhere, you have not seen anything. What do you know about the mountains? What I said is true. That is marron country. The people up there escaped from the whites during slavery times. They were the brave ones. Even before the Revolution they made war against the French. The French sent troops to recapture or kill them, but they could not do it. Those people fought with spears because they did not have guns, but they drove the French back running. Yes, the cemetery is there, and so are other things I saw. This young man will get home swiftly if he listens to me. Many vodouns have reposoirs up there, more than here. The loa General Brisé, you'll find him living in a chardette tree. That's his reposoir. Before you cut a chardette tree down you have to have a service to make sure Brisé isn't resting in it. There aren't many crabs up there, but if you find one you have to make sure Papa Bambara isn't resting inside. I think the vodouns like the mountains because it's quieter there than down here by the ocean. Instead of going home to Guinée they sometimes go to the high mountains. Then if we call them they don't have so far to travel." He looked at me sharply. "Some of those loa are pretty stern. You have to be careful. Also there are plenty of bakas."

I said, "Thank you for telling me, Papa." He said, "I don't think you understand much about loa and bakas." I said, "Papa, I know a little about loa, but we generally call them vodouns." He said, "Yes, yes, the same. Do you have a head-spirit?" I answered, "Yes, Ogoun." He exclaimed, "Ah! That is a good loa to have. I almost had Ogoun for my head-spirit. I thought he was Ogoun, but he turned out to be Agwé instead. When he rode me the first time my houngan called him Ogoun and it made him angry. Agwé was so angry he threw me around hard and frightened everyone out of the service. My houngan had to make a special ceremony to placate Papa Agwé. Since then, though, Agwé has taken good care of me." I was interested in what the old man was telling me, but I wanted to be on the trail. As I left the crossroads market an old woman said to me in a quiet voice, "Do not think everything he said about the trail is true. He may be right, but he forgets and mixes things up." I thanked her and started walking across the marshy flats.

I hadn't gone far when I heard the old man calling me. He was walking as fast as he could on the wet, slippery ground, and sometimes his cane sank deep in the soft earth and he had to stop and pull it out. When he caught up to me he was breathing heavily. He said, "People don't believe some things I tell them, but that is because they are all children and have not seen much of life. What I want to tell you is to be wary of bakas and demons in those mountains, especially the bakulus, which resemble pieces of morning mist. Often they look like people, and you don't recognize them until it is too late. Sometimes they seem to be a line of market women walking along the trail. If they catch you they suck all the moisture from your body. If you have a good protective garde, be sure to wear it. There are also

toy, some were jumping around with carved wooden zozos between their legs and making thrusting motions as if they were copulating, and all the while new ones were pushing their way out of the ground.

I found myself lurching this way and that, and my head felt as if everything in the world were inside it. Whether I was dancing or singing or lying on the ground I did not know, but at a certain moment I had the sensation of being held by the feet and being whipped around in the air. There was great commotion among the Gèdés, some running one way, some another, and I became unconscious. When I awoke I was very weak, as if I had just been born, and everything was quiet. Little by little I became aware of the sky, the trees, and the other things around me. The shrine was still there but all the Gèdés had disappeared. I sat up and discovered I was holding in my hand the piece of iron Kuku Cabrit had given me. Then I understood that my maît′ tête, my protector Ogoun, had come to my aid and entered my head, battled with the Gèdés and driven them out.

Though the Gèdés were lords of death, Ogoun was a fierce warrior who would not tolerate their taking possession of his reposoir. When my strength returned I said, "Thank you Papa, thank you Ogoun of the sword and iron, thank you for protecting me." And I sang a song to him which I continued to sing for a long while as I walked unsteadily along the trail:

> *Ogoun oh,*
> *Great man of the forge.*
> *Ogoun oh,*
> *Iron flows from his hands.*
> *Ogoun oh,*
> *His buttons and stirrups are iron.*
> *Ogoun oh,*
> *Poisoned food cannot kill his horse.*

That song came to be a permanent bond between me and Ogoun. In later days if it was sung at a service, or if the drums merely played the appropriate beat, Ogoun would come into the peristyle where a service was taking place and enter my head immediately. The houngan would put a red military jacket on me at once and place a sword in my hand and I would do all the things a person possessed by Ogoun is supposed to do. Everyone called me Papa or addressed me by one of Ogoun's praise names.

I journeyed through the mountains several more days. Sometimes I could see the sea down below, and once I saw Port-au-Prince and the lakes in the Cul-de-Sac Plain where my grandfather Djalan lived when he first became a marron, before he came up above and made his permanent habitation in the mountains. Every morning I thanked Ogoun for his protection, and I never passed a crossroad or took a new trail without asking Legba to keep me from losing my way. My joy was great when I met a small boy who told me Dleau Frète was not more than a day's journey ahead.

That night I slept deeply, but I felt depressed when I awoke because of a vivid dream in which my father came and talked to me. He said, "I am well down here in Yzolé Below the Water. I have watched you during your long and dangerous journey to Habitation Perdue. Your grandfather Djalan also has been watching you. You will reach home safely. Take care of your mother. Also, it is time for you to find yourself a wife so that you can have children and, in time, be an ancestor in your own right. But do not forget that there is something urgent that still has to be done." I said, "Yes, Papa, tell me what it is."

He said, "You were at my déssounin when my head-spirit was liberated. You saw me accuse a certain man of sending an expedition against me. His name is Alsandor. I had many years ahead. But Alsandor believed I had caused the maize in his garden to wither and his bull to fall from a cliff. He went to a bocor in Léogane by the name of Basfort and paid him a great deal of money for an expedition against me. With his right hand, Basfort served the loas, the vodouns, and with his left hand he performed vindictive magic. Basfort worked with his left hand against me. He sent a disease that ate my living substance. I did not know it at the time I became ill. When Kuku Cabrit was beginning to remove Hevioso from my head I still did not know it. It was Hevioso himself who stood my body up and searched out Alsandor and pointed my finger at him. All this I have learned only since arriving at Yzolé Below the Water. You are my oldest son, therefore it is you who must do something." The dream lingered on even when I was walking again on the trail. I wondered what I could do to punish Alsandor. At last I decided to stop thinking about it and wait until I could talk to Kuku Cabrit, since he would know about such things.

Late in the afternoon I began to recognize certain peaks and hills, and I asked everyone who passed if I was on the right way to Dleau Frète. Everyone said yes, and I was elated. Before long I was in the center of the village among the produce vendors and buyers. It was difficult to believe I was really there after all that time in the wilderness. I did not think I could feel any happier. But then I saw Jean-Jacques and a member of his work society coming to meet me. We embraced and said all kinds of foolish things. They had a knapsack full of food and we sat under a tree and ate. People lingered nearby and greeted me, or just exclaimed "Woy!" over and over again as if I were the president, but I'm sure they didn't really know where I had been or where I was going. I think all they knew was that Jean-Jacques and his friend had been watching and waiting for me and at last I had arrived.

Eventually it occurred to me to ask my brother how he knew I was coming. Jean-Jacques said that several days earlier Kuku Cabrit had been holding a service at his hounfor, and that a number of head-spirits had made their appearance. The next morning he came up the mountain and told my mother he had been informed I was approaching Dleau Frète but could not say how close I might be. My brother and his friend left as soon as possible and had been waiting in Dleau Frète for two days.

There was a moment when none of us was talking, and I felt as if someone was staring at my back to attract my attention. I turned and saw the house with the cashew tree, and sitting at the door smoking a pipe was someone I knew, Mama Délina Lafleur. She pretended not to be watching me, though I knew she was. Délina Lafleur, who had sent me up Justin's trail and told me to turn off into the gully at the place where a white strip of cloth was tied to a tree. I became angry, because that was the time all my bad ordeals had begun, and I was sure she had intended it that way. She had put a force in motion that led me from one ordeal to another. Yet I was not completely certain. Had not my trail taken me, in the end, to Habitation Perdue?

I arose and went to her house without knowing what I wanted to say to her. She said, "Dosu Bordeaux, you are here." I answered awkwardly, "Yes, Mama, I have come back." She said, "It was a cruel journey." I answered, "Yes, Mama." She said, "You believe I was the one who caused your miseries?" I did not speak the way I felt. I said, "No, Mama." She said, "Dosu, it was not I. You wanted something. You wanted to go somewhere. Someone else could have given you bad advice, and you might have died without accomplishing anything. I was not sure you would survive. But you wanted to go on the journey. I did not suggest it. I am not a houngan or a bocor or a mambo, but I have a gift of sight. I directed you to the point in space where your journey had to begin, the tree with the white strip of cloth. If you had not gone there, who knows where you would be today? Everything that happened to you after that was a link in a chain that led you to Habitation Perdue. I was not responsible for anything but sending you to the magic point where everything began." I listened silently and she went on.

"Think about what I said." She reached into her thatched roof and brought out a cloth in which some coins were wrapped. She counted out thirty-five cob and put them on the bench by the door. She said, "If I cheated you or brought you to any harm, here are the thirty-five cob you gave me for my clear-seeing. Take them back and forget we ever met." I was overcome with shame that I had blamed Délina Lafleur for any of my misfortunes. I excused myself and went to where my brother was waiting, and I asked him for all the coins he had in his pocket. We counted them out and they added up to seven gourdes, which I took back to Délina Lafleur. I placed them on the bench next to the thirty-five cob.

I said, "Mama, excuse me for everything. When I came through here before and you looked into the future for me I was very inexperienced. I did not understand things. But since then

I have learned much. I know now that you helped me on my way. If not for you I might never have reached my destination. I thank you and wish you a long and prosperous life. I will always remember you for your help, and so will my brother Jean-Jacques." She did not say anything, but I could see in her face that she was gratified.

XVIII

My brother and his friend and I stayed in Dleau Frète that night and set out for home early the next morning when the mist was still thick. We stopped at Kuku Cabrit's house, but he was not there. One of his grandchildren told us he had gone to my mother's place. We arrived in the afternoon and as we went up the path to my mother's house it appeared at first that there was no one home. Then suddenly my brother's work society emerged from a grove of trees in a noisy perambulating dance, all wearing their festive costumes. There were jongleurs wearing great horned headdresses and sequined shirts, and behind them a man carried the society's banner. Musicians played bamboo trumpets, conch horns and drums, and everyone was singing:

Dosu Bordeaux arrives, he arrives!
Oh Dosu Bordeaux arrives at last!
We cry, "Welcome Brother Dosu,
Welcome at last to Dosu Bordeaux!"

They moved around us in a wide circle, some of them performing acrobatic tricks. A man representing vodoun Azaka or Cousin appeared from somewhere on tall stilts, but he stumbled on the stones and fell into the crowd.

I went where my mother was crying in the doorway of the house and she clung to me as if I were going to be snatched away. Quite a few people were inside, including Kuku Cabrit, Jean-Jacques' wife, and my sisters. It was a fine celebration. That night there was a dance in the courtyard in honor of all our protective vodouns, including above all Ogoun, Azaka, and Hevioso. Three drummers from the Habitation of Beautiful Pines brought their drums and the dancing went on nearly all night. By early morning quite a few people were sleeping on benches or on the ground wherever they could find room, or sitting up in chairs propped against the house. Finally Kuku Cabrit called out "Abobo!" signifying that the celebration had come to an end.

I slept a long sleep and did not get up until the sun was overhead. My mother gave me coffee and bread, after which I went out and inspected her gardens and the spring. Jean-Jacques' work society had cared for everything perfectly and there was nothing for me to do at the moment. They had even gathered a large supply of firewood. So I spent the rest of the day making repairs to the house. My sisters did not really live in the house any longer, being married and having children, but they stayed with my mother and helped her with pestling grain, winnowing, sweeping, and other household activities. They all kept asking questions about the journey, and I told them a few things but did not really feel like talking about it very much. The previous night I had been mounted by Ogoun. Kuku Cabrit had monitored my possession and sent Ogoun away when it was time for him to go, but the possession had left me feeling listless. In addition, though the celebration had been a fine one, I missed my father and felt depressed about my obligation to see that the man named Alsandor was repaid for his evil work.

I did not speak of the matter to any of my family, but five or six days later I went down to visit Kuku Cabrit. I told him many of the things that had happened to me and he listened intently. I told him of my grandfather Djalan coming to get me for my father's déssounin, and asked him if I was really there. He said, "Yes, Dosu, you were really here." I told him also of the dream when my father came to me and told me all about Alsandor, and I asked if he knew all about these things. He said, "Yes, Dosu, it was really your father speaking to you, and what he told you was true." At last I said, "Now I know for certain I must do something, but I don't know how to begin."

Kuku Cabrit said, "I have been thinking about the matter for some time. Your father was my good friend. I know that in Izolé Below the Water he has been waiting patiently for something to be done about Alsandor. But where is Alsandor now? People would not speak to him. If they saw him coming they stepped off the trail until he passed. The blacksmith in Dleau Frète would not repair his hoe for him. If Alsandor's wife tried to buy something from a vendor, the vendor threw a cloth over her tray and turned her back. One day Alsandor stood in the middle of Dleau Frète shouting that people were unjust to him, that he hadn't had anything to do with your father's death and, besides, Jérémie Bordeaux was an evil man, a baka who had caused Alsandor's bull to fall over a cliff, and made his maize dry up in the garden. Not only that, he said Jérémie had made the rain pass by his habitation when it was raining everywhere else. He said the people of Dleau Frète must all be devils to treat him in such a bad manner. A few days after that Alsandor and his family deserted his habitation. No one saw him go. It is not known who did it, but someone went there in the night and burned his house down so that people would not have to look at it any more."

Kuku Cabrit was quiet for a while, and I waited for him to go on. Then he said, "Everyone knows the truth about Alsandor. Still, before doing something strong we must not overlook anything. Therefore I went to the ruins of Alsandor's house with my gembo and I asked questions. I said, 'Did a baka kill Jérémie?' The gembo was motionless, meaning no. I asked, 'Was Jérémie killed by an expedition?' The shell slid downwards on the cord, meaning yes. I asked if Alsandor was responsible, and the shell slid again and became agitated. I asked many questions. We know for certain about Alsandor.

"But for what we are going to do we need a special kind of bocor. I am a houngan, I work with my right hand to serve the vodouns. There are others who are both houngans and bocors. They serve vodouns with the right hand and make magic with the left. They are not strong enough. There are others who are 'left-handed,' which is to say they serve only with the left hand. There is no defense against their expeditions.

"There is a certain left-handed bocor who resides on the route to Léogane. He is very strong. His name is Bocor Danpisse. It is said that he cut off his right hand to give more power to his left. He lives in a cave known as Trou Dantor. Mostly he works with vodouns of the Congo-Pétro nation. If you want to ask him for help, I will go with you. But you will have to pay him a great deal. I can't say how much he will demand. All I know is that if an ordinary bocor might ask for a chicken, he will ask for ten. If an ordinary bocor would ask for a calf, he will ask for a cow. If an ordinary bocor would ask for five gourdes in silver, Bocor Danpisse will demand fifty."

I said I did not have a great deal of anything, but I would try to get it. When I returned from Kuku Cabrit's place I went to my brother's house and told him about the matter. Jean-Jacques said he was involved as much as I was and he would find the money. Three days later he came to my house, strictly speaking my mother's house, and gave me a small bundle wrapped in a kerchief. He said, "There are twenty-seven of us in the Habitation of the Beautiful Pines. Everyone gave something because you saved me from the zombie plantation." I opened the kerchief and found many bills and coins. After that my mother went to a corner of the room, removed a mat from the ground and dug out another packet of coins. She said, "Your father buried these coins here. I know he wants you to have them." This was the way I acquired the money I needed for Bocor Danpisse.

Several days later Kuku Cabrit and I began our journey. From Dleau Frète there was a well-used trail toward Léogane. Kuku Cabrit made a brief service for Legba before we left the village, and whenever we passed a cross-trail he asked Legba to keep our road smooth and without accident. The next morning at a spot where the mountain was beginning to level off into the Léogane plain we came to a large banyan tree. The trail to the cave, Trou Dantor, branched off at this place, and we recognized it easily because of the objects hanging in the tree branches. Anyone would know Bocor Danpisse lived there. There were bundles of feathers, grave diggers' tools, a human skull, a dead goat, several chicken heads and lizards' tails, and around the trunk was a circle of whitewashed stones. It was not far to the cave where Danpisse lived. It had a wooden door, above which were the insignia, painted in white, of several Congo-Pétro vodouns, as well as some designs Kuku Cabrit had never seen before.

He knocked on the door with his baton, but there was no response from inside. He knocked again, and this time the door flew open and an old man wearing a leather shirt came out. He did not greet us, but stood staring. Kuku Cabrit addressed him politely, saying we had come a long distance to consult Bocor Danpisse on a matter of importance. The man said, "Well, I am Danpisse. What do you want?" Kuku Cabrit introduced himself, noting that he himself was a houngan. They shook hands in a peculiar way, first palm to palm, then shifting to grasp each other's thumbs, then wrists, in this manner showing their credentials. Bocor Danpisse went inside, returning with a long rope whip called a frète cache which he lashed seven times in front of the doorway, after which he invited us to enter. Kuku Cabrit told me later that the lashing of the frète cache was to call to order all the various baka, demons, and spirits under Danpisse's control. Danpisse sat in a chair and we sat on a bench facing him. The walls of the room were covered with designs, vèvès, rattles, and banners of various kinds, and on a table in one corner there were carved wooden figures and seven or eight govies containing head-spirits. In another corner a number of drums were stacked against the wall. Danpisse lighted a pine torch and I noticed for the first time that his right hand was missing at the wrist. I was not very comfortable about being in this place and began to have misgivings. I did not like

Bocor Danpisse. And I began to wonder why Kuku Cabrit himself had not volunteered to do the work. After all, he was my father's friend.

Kuku Cabrit explained why we had come and asked if Danpisse would be willing to locate Alsandor and launch an expedition as punishment for the killing of my father. Danpisse said he knew about the crime and the participation of a certain bocor in Léogane. He said it would be possible to divine, with wari beans, Alsandor's present location. That would be the easy part. Recruiting a vodoun or baka to carry out the expedition would be more difficult. It would cost money, not for Danpisse's pocket but for conducting services that would determine if an appropriate spirit would agree to be involved. "Some vodouns will not agree to do certain things," he said. "If a vodoun is connected in any way with the family of the doomed person, he will not accept the commission. Things must be bought for use in the inquest ceremony. Because you are a fellow practitioner in the mystical arts, I will make a very special price to the young man. One hundred gourdes."

Kuku Cabrit asked me how much money I had. I took out my packet of bills and coins and counted them. I felt very disappointed. I did not have nearly a hundred gourdes. Kuku Cabrit took the money and counted it again. He said to Danpisse, "He has only seventy-two gourdes and twenty centimes. Bocor Danpisse shrugged his shoulders and said, "Well, in that case I cannot help you." Kuku Cabrit stood up, saying, "I am sorry for that. Then we will have to go on to Léogane." He motioned to me to follow him and started out the door. But Danpisse called him back, saying, "It is a long way to Léogane. I would like to save you the journey. I will accept the seventy-two gourdes and twenty centimes, but of course we will have to eliminate some aspects of the ceremony." Kuku Cabrit said, "But if you eliminate anything essential we may not succeed, and Dosu's money will be wasted."

Danpisse said, "I will eliminate carefully, nothing that will affect the outcome." Kuku Cabrit said, "I want to be sure that you accept this matter with full responsibility, and that the expedition will be successful in every way." Danpisse answered as though offended, saying, "Do you doubt my word that Al-sandor will be taken care of?" Kuku Cabrit said, "No one can doubt the word of Bocor Danpisse. I just want to make sure that we have heard the word." Danpisse said, "Yes, yes, you have heard it." Kuku Cabrit motioned for me to give Danpisse the money, which I did. Danpisse put the money in a wooden box, then called for his wife, whom we had not yet seen, to bring us coffee. She came out of a back room of the cave with three china cups of coffee. We drank our coffee without referring again to our business. When we were finished, Bocor Danpisse said, "Tonight I will divine Alsandor's whereabouts, and tomorrow we will go on from there." We thanked him and left. When we were outside the cave, Bocor Danpisse again took up his frète cache and lashed seven times in front of the doorway. Kuku Cabrit told me that this was to drive the head-spirits back into their govies in case they had attempted to escape while we were talking.

We found a place to stay that night with an elderly woman who lived a short distance away. As I had given up all the money I possessed, Kuku Cabrit paid for our keep. I should have felt good because we had succeeded in making our ar-rangements but instead I felt distressed. I did not think Dan-pisse was a good man, and I suddenly realized that what I was arranging with him was the actual killing of a person. I had known it all the time, of course, but I somehow had not known it completely until I had entered Trou Dantor and listened to Danpisse talking about the money. Alsandor deserved to be punished for what he did to my father, but Danpisse did not seem to care about that part of it. It seemed to me that it would have been the same to him if we had been discussing the killing of a child or a chicken.

I asked Kuku Cabrit why he himself was not sending the expedition. I reminded him that he had sent an expedition to France when my grandfather's enemy caused his well to dry up, and that he had been successful. Kuku Cabrit said, "Dosu, this is a different kind of matter. The expedition I sent was to torture Djalan's enemy until he reversed the magic he had launched and Djalan's spring flowed again. It was a protective expedition to undo something bad that had been done. This time it is far more serious. It will not bring your father back. It will not undo anything. It is fierce attack magic. I cannot do it because my profession is only to serve the vodouns." Hearing that, I felt more distressed than before. I said, "Will this expedition help my father in any way?" He said, "No, it will not change his life in Yzolé Below the Water. Everything will remain the same for him except that he will feel he has received the justice to which he is entitled."

I asked if something else could be done to Alsandor besides killing him. Could Danpisse send him a disease of some kind, or shrivel his arms or legs? Kuku Cabrit said, "Danpisse specializes in strong remedies. But we will sleep on it and tomorrow we will discuss it with him. Perhaps tomorrow you will not feel the same way." Already I felt ashamed for suggesting that perhaps Alsandor should not be killed. I knew he should be killed. After all, he had killed my father. No punishment could be too strong for that. My determination returned. Anything that could be done to Alsandor would be done. Yet I remained depressed.

That night I had many vivid dreams, one sliding into another. I dreamed about Habitation Perdue, and about the Gèdé shrine in the valley with all the Gèdés prancing about, and Ogoun coming into my head to drive Gèdé away. It was frightening and I felt very helpless. Then these pictures faded away and I was talking to my father. He put his hand on my shoulder and said, "Do not be afraid, Dosu. It will be all right." I said, "Papa, I am not afraid. I will see that Alsandor is punished." He said, "Yes, I know what you are doing." I said, "Papa, if I did not do it I would be ashamed to return home." He smiled at me, and that gave me a happy feeling. He said, "Do not worry any more. Everything is taken care of. Alsandor has already been punished by the vodoun Sonponno. Sonponno sent him the smallpox and he died yesterday. They could not bury him in the graveyard, because anyone killed by Sonponno cannot be buried there. His body was wrapped in his sleeping mat and thrown into a deep gully. There is nothing more for you to do." My father's face slowly faded away and I awoke trembling.

I awakened Kuku Cabrit at once and I told him my father had come and spoken to me. I said Alsandor was already dead. I told him everything I could remember of my dream, everything my father had said. He took the oil lamp down from where it was hanging and held it close to my face. He asked, "Was it only a dream, an ordinary dream, or did Jérémie really come?" I said, "I was sleeping, but my father was there. He was very real." He asked me to tell him again who it was that sent the sickness to Alsandor, and I said, "Sonponno." He asked me who Sonponno was and I said I did not know, I had never heard of him before. Kuku Cabrit said, "You have never heard of Sonponno?" I shook my head. He put the lamp down on the floor and said. "Then I believe it was really your father who was talking to you, otherwise how could you have heard the name? Sonponno is an ancient Guinée vodoun. He is responsible for smallpox, but we do not hear much about him any more. Once when I was a young boy I was at a harvest feast and Sonponno entered a man's head. The man died of smallpox two days later. In all the years since that time I have not often heard Sonponno mentioned. He is not among the vodouns we serve. In the morning we will discuss it with Bocor Danpisse."

Filled with the vivid memory of my father's visit, I did not sleep any more that night. The sun rose and the woman gave us a little coffee, and after that we returned to Danpisse's place. He lashed his frète cache before the door and invited us in. He began to speak of the things he would have to do to launch the expedition. Kuku Cabrit said, "It will not be necessary. Alsandor has just died." Danpisse was startled. He said, "How can you know that?" Kuku Cabrit said, "Dosu's father came in the night and told Dosu." Danpisse said, "Ah, he dreamed something?" Kuku Cabrit said, "No, his father spoke of Sonponno." Now Bocor Danpisse was very alert. His face was serious. He thought for a while, then said, "I will check it with my Guinée beans."

He took a packet from a closed calabash container and sat on the floor. After clearing the dust away with his hand, he opened the packet and spilled thirty-six Guinée beans on the ground. They were similar to our Haitian wari beans, but larger and black rather than red. He closed his eyes and recited something in a low voice, invoking a long list of vodouns, many of whom were strange to me. Then he scraped the Guinée beans together with the blade of his machete, picked them up and threw them again. After reading them he made a mark on the ground with his finger and again threw them down. He kept throwing the Guinée beans and making marks. He threw thirty-six times. After that he studied the marks carefully. They seemed to be telling him something. He began a new series of marks. This went on for a long time, and after that he seemed to sleep, with his chin on his chest. A short time later he started talking a strange language. At last it was over. He brushed the Guinée beans aside and said, "Yes, he is dead. It was Sonponno."

Kuku Cabrit said, "You confirm it?" He answered, "Yes, I confirm it." Kuku Cabrit said, "In that case we do not need the expedition." Bocor Danpisse said, "No, we do not need it." He went to the box where he kept his money and took out some bills and handed them to Kuku Cabrit, who said, "That is not enough. The expedition was the expensive part. Give Dosu back half of what he gave you." Danpisse became angry, and almost immediately a vodoun entered his head. He threw himself about the room violently. Kuku Cabrit said to me, "Let us go. The money doesn't matter now." We went out of the cave and began our journey home.

That is the end of the story I wanted to tell about certain things that happened when I was young. I am an old man now, but I will be glad if anyone reads what M. Morancy has set down on paper and gets to know about those experiences just the way they occurred. When my mother died, I moved away from our habitation, and my brother Jean-Jacques came back and settled there because of my grandfather Djalan's wonderful spring. Jean-Jacques is still living and the spring is still flowing. Also, sometimes he hears the voices of our ancestors bubbling up in the water. On my present habitation I grow many kinds of crops—yams, pumpkins, plantains, maize, and millet. I also have good coco-palms and mango and avocado trees. My head-spirit, Ogoun, has stayed with me and helped me in difficult times. Every so often my father Jérémie or my grandfather Djalan comes to talk with me when I am sleeping to keep me encouraged. My wife weaves straw hats and baskets, and she is very good at commerce. Her name is Félicie.

She is the same Félicie, Félicie Moreau, from that fishing village I passed through during my journey to Habitation Perdue. Even though she had rejected me because I would not stay with her and be a fisherman, I never stopped thinking about her. About six months after I returned home I had a dream that Félicie was standing on a trail somewhere waiting for me. In the morning I put on my best clothes and started out for her village. This time I went down to Léogane and took the sea road. When I arrived she was in front of her house pestling grain. I told her to gather her belongings because we would be going back to the Red Mountains in three days. This time she did not make things difficult and didn't complain that I knew nothing about fishing or mending a net. The night before we left there was a big celebration in the village that lasted almost until dawn.

There is just one more thing and then I will be finished. While we were on the road back to Léogane I saw a man coming toward us riding a donkey. Even at a distance there was something familiar about him. Before he reached us I recognized him as the white bocor who had burned my protective passport and made me say, "Father, Son and Holy Spirit." He was wearing his black robe and a black hat, one of his feet was dragging on the ground, and he was carrying a black book. There was a cord around the donkey's neck with a cross hanging from it. At first I thought of getting off the road into the brush where he could not see me. But I didn't want Félicie to observe me doing that, so I just looked straight ahead. When he passed us and was some distance away, I turned and spoke the words Kuku Cabrit had given me for invoking Legba: "Agoé, Agola, Agochi!"

At that very moment his donkey brayed, put its head down, and kicked its heels high in the air. The white bocor went up and then landed all sprawled out on the road. The market women nearby put their hands over their mouths to smother their laughing. After that they helped him back on his donkey. I made Legba's mark on the ground with my finger and said, "Merci Papa, Master of the Highway! Merci, Attibon!" Of course Legba could have done much worse to him, but he was in a lighthearted mood.

Glossary

ABIKU
: In Yoruba tradition (carried over to some of the Caribbean cultures) an infant or young child who dies and is later reborn, usually to the same parents.

ABOBO
: A sign-off word used to indicate the end of a dance, an invocation, or a song.

AGOÉ! AGOLA! AGOCHI!
: An untranslatable phrase sometimes used to end a ritual.

AGWÉ
: A vodoun, or loa, of the sea.

AKASAN
: A broth made of ground corn, often eaten in thicker form resembling porridge.

ANASACO
: Title of the doctor or diviner of the Egbo fraternal society of the Ekoi and Efik peoples of West Africa. The society survived in some Caribbean communities, most notably in Cuba.

ASSON
: A small rattle, with a network of beads on the outside, used ritually by houngans and mambos.

AZAKA
: The special vodoun, or loa, of country people. Often referred to as Cousin.

BAKA
: An evil supernatural being that preys on humans. It can take on a variety of grotesque forms or resemble ordinary people.

185

BAKULU   A form of demon.

BAMBARA   An African tribe. Also the name of a vodoun, or
                  loa, believed to be of Bambara origin.

BIZANGO   A predatory demon resembling a large black dog,
                  believed to frequent the back country in search of
                  human prey.

BOCOR   A cult priest who specializes in aggressive or de-
                  structive magic. Said to work with his left hand,
                  in contrast to the houngan, who works with his
                  right hand and whose primary role is to assist
                  and guide people of his hounfor in their relations
                  with the vodouns. See HOUNGAN.

BON-ANGE   Haitians differ as to the exact nature of the bon-
                  ange (frequently called the gros bon-ange to dis-
                  tinguish it from the petit bon-ange), though in
                  general it is regarded as the basic inner spirit
                  with which every individual is born. In transla-
                  tion, it is referred to in this narrative as "soul
                  spirit."

BOSSALE   Wild, free, "untamed."

BRISÉ   The name of a vodoun, or loa, belonging to the
                  Congo-Pétro group.

CACIQUE   Leader, chief.

CAILLE   House, in particular a small peasant house made
                  of wattle and lime with a thatch or tin roof. Also
                  the Haitian name of the African game best
                  known as mankala or owari. In Haiti, as in Af-
                  rica, the gameboard and playing pieces were
                  sometimes used for divining.

COCOMACAQUE   Literally, "monkey palm." A diminutive palm tree
                  from which walking sticks, thought to have the
                  power to repel bakas, were made.

COMPÈRE — Godfather. Used as a familiar term of respect among older persons.

CONGO MAPIONGLE — The name of a vodoun of the Congo-Pétro group.

CONNAISSANCE — Special understanding, usually of the vodouns and rituals of the hounfor.

COUMBITE — A cooperative agricultural work group whose members help one another in farming tasks.

DÉSSOUNIN — The rite of removing a vodoun from the head of a deceased person.

DIFÉ — Fire. Often used to designate the pot of embers carried by mountain people so they may make a fire when needed.

EGBO — An important secret fraternal society of the Efik and Ekoi peoples of West Africa.

EXPEDITION — Aggressive magic by which a bocor sends a spirit to neutralize or harm an enemy.

ENGAGEMENT — A compact made with a vodoun, a bocor, or any practitioner of magic.

FILELIKELA — Bambara term designating a diviner.

FRÈTE CACHE — The cracking of a long whip by a bocor or houngan to attract the attention of a vodoun, or loa, or to give force to magical pronouncements or actions.

GANGAN — Synonymous with houngan, a vodoun priest.

GARDE CORPS — A charm worn on the body for protection against evil or accident.

GEMBO

A divining device used by houngans, made of a shell that slides on a taut string.

GOVI

An earthen jar or jug in which a houngan keeps various kinds of spirits, including a loa removed from a dead person's head.

GÈDÉ

Known under various names such as Baron Samedi, Gèdé Nimbo, Brave Gèdé, Baron Cimitière, etc. The vodoun of the graveyard, or death. Characterized by incivility, crude behavior, contempt for rules.

GUINÉE

Africa.

HABITANT

A peasant farmer or landholder.

HABITATION

A peasant house and landholding.

HEVIOSO

Sometimes pronounced Kébioso. A Dahomean sky vodoun who, like Shango of the Yoruba, hurls thunderbolts at the earth. Indian stone adzes found by country people are regarded as thunder stones thrown by Hevioso, Sobo, or Shango.

HOUNGAN

A cult priest devoted to serving the vodouns, or loa. He generally performs rituals with his right hand. A houngan who performs aggressive magic is said to "work with two hands," while a bocor is described as one who "works with his left hand."

HOUNFOR

The main building or building complex of a houngan.

IFA

The divining orisha (equivalent to vodoun) of the West African Yoruba people. Also called Orunmila. Though he is scarcely recalled by name in Haiti, Ifa divining, in simplified form, survived.

The Ifa tray is the board on which divining was performed.

IMAMOU
The generic name for Haitian vodouns of the sea. Some persons describe Imamou as the paramount sea vodoun, though the best known of sea vodouns is Agwé. Vèvès for Agwé usually show a sailing ship with the name Imamou drawn on its side.

LACOUR
A small group of huts occupied by members of an extended family.

LEGBA
The vodoun, or loa, of the gateway, the highway, and the crossroads.

LOA
Another word for vodoun. See VODOUN.

LOUGARO
Loup garou. A demon-like creature that can take on various forms to prey on humans.

MOUNDONGUE
A vodoun, or loa, associated with Congo-Pétro rites. The name of a tribe in Central Africa.

MAÎT' GRAND BOIS
Master of the Forest, the supreme vodoun of the forest or wilderness.

MAMBO
A priestess who conducts vodoun rites.

MARRON
In colonial times, an escaped slave. Marrons often gathered in the mountains and built villages or established individual homesteads.

MARASSA
Twin, twins. A vodoun named Marassa is the special protector of twins.

MAWU
In Dahomey, Mawu or Mawu-Lissa was regarded as a very ancient deity and progenitor of the other vodouns.

MAYAMBA
A chip-tossing gambling game.

NANANBOUCLOU In Dahomey Nananbouclou is considered to be the most ancient, the original, vodoun, the parent of Mawu (Mawu-Lissa). In Haiti he (or she) is sometimes called Nananbélécou.

OGOUN The vodoun of iron and war, as among the Yoruba of Nigeria.

OLORUN The paramount sky spirit or deity of the Yoruba of Nigeria.

OUANGA A charm made by a bocor for aggressive, harmful magic against a certain individual. Sometimes the charm is not actually made in material form but only vocalized in ritual language.

PAR-PRETÉ A trade of food or other objects in exchange for labor.

PASSAGE D'ALLIANCE A method of divining to establish the identity or guilt of a person.

PERISTYLE The roofed court adjoining a hounfor.

PIED COUPÉ A vodoun with one leg, or a one-legged baka, who lives in a certain tree and preys on human passers-by.

PINGA MAZA A fearsome vodoun of the Congo-Pétro group.

PLACÉE Under the sanctioned tradition of plaçage, a man who already has one wife and household may take a second wife to care for another house and garden some distance away. She is said to be placée. In the Haitian peasant setting she is not necessarily held to be inferior to the first wife.

REPOSOIR A "resting place" for a vodoun. It can be a tree, a rock, a cave, or sometimes a person's head.

SAMBA A community story teller, amateur or professional, who entertains children or adults on special occasions.

SHANGO
A Haitian vodoun of Yoruba origin.

SOCIÉTÉ
A men's or women's group organized for a specific purpose, such as communal labor or affiliation with a particular hounfor.

SONPONNO
A Vodoun of Yoruba origin. Among the Yoruba he was considered the spirit/deity of smallpox and other such diseases.

TAFIA
An alcoholic beverage made from sugar cane.

TAINO
An Indian tribe or subtribe that occupied parts of Haiti before the arrival of Europeans.

THUNDER STONE
In traditional Haitian belief, certain Indian stone artifacts, particularly hand adzes, found during agricultural work are thunder stones hurled by the vodoun Hevioso or the vodoun Shango. They are highly valued and are displayed on special ritual occasions.

TIJEAN PÉTRO
A Pétro vodoun or loa who, in traditional Haitian belief, preys on humans, particularly children, from the foliage of the coconut palm.

TONNELLE
The covering of the courtyard adjoining a hounfor.

VÈVÈ
A corn meal drawing or design made on the earth by a houngan during a ceremony or ritual service.

VODOUN
A Dahomean (Fon) term designating any of the deities or spirit beings worshipped, placated, or served in Afro-Haitian religious rites. In Dahomey these spirit beings belonged to sky, earth, and sea pantheons, a distinction no longer ob-

served in Haiti, though they still have functions related to sky, sea, and earth. Services for vodouns are generically called Vodoun. In contemporary Haiti the word *Vodoun* is used to indicate, collectively, Vodoun religion in all its aspects, and the word *loa* is most commonly used to designate the deities themselves.

WARI

A large red seed (referred to by Haitians as a pois or bean) used for various purposes such as bleaching skin, poisoning, playing pieces for the game of caille, and divining.

YZOLÉ

One of various names for the under-the-water residing place of deceased persons. It is believed by some that vodouns also live there.

ZANDOLITE

A small tree lizard.

ZAGOUTI

A mammal about the size of a rabbit, related to the guinea pig.

ZEAUBEAUP

According to tradition, a society of cannibals.

ZOMBIE

Explained at length in the narrative.